SNAKES IN THE MIX

THE MIXED GIRL SERIES BOOK THREE

LAMONIQUE MAC

For information email: lamoniquemac@themixedgirlseries.com

Cover Design by: Terry Cooper

ISBN: 978-17354287-5-8 (paperback)

To the overcomers before they've overcame.

Be not overcome of evil, but overcome evil with good.

— ROMANS 12:21

ALSO BY LAMONIQUE MAC

The Mixed Girl Series

Poor Little Mixed Girl (Book One)

Mixed Out (Book Two)

Snakes in the Mix (Book Three)

SIGN UP FOR MY NEWSLETTER

Be the first to learn about LaMonique Mac's new releases and receive exclusive content for fiction readers.

www.authorlamoniquemac.com

JUST KICKIN' IT

L aMonica and Marciana were riding down the street on the bumpy bus ride home from Flint to Saginaw. They were both grappling with the fact that Programming Systems Institute (PSI) was closing its doors because of Financial Aid fraud. The government was shutting them down.

LaMonica was wringing her hands while in deep thought. Not having a school to attend would have serious implications for her. In order to keep her job at the courthouse through the Job Training Partnership Act (JTPA), she was required to be enrolled in school. Without that weekly check, having money to take care of her daughter Monica would be extremely hard.

Not to mention, school and her internship were the only places she felt like she was excelling in life. Bishop was constantly reminding her she's just a "teeny bopper" and not a "real woman" because of her lack of organization at home.

Earlier that day, the ride to PSI had been so much more carefree before they got the big news from school. Marciana had a Walkman with a cassette tape by the music group Xscape playing. She was enraptured in the music, singing along while rolling her neck from side to side with her arms outstretched like she was attending a concert. In a bubbly voice she asked, "Hey LaMonica do you want to listen?"

"Who's playing? It must be good because you're over there having a good time."

"It's Xscape."

Marciana's enthusiasm was infectious. "Oh yeah. I love their new song," LaMonica said.

"Yeah, yeah, yeah, I know the one you're talking about. The one they play on the radio all the time. What's it called?"

"*Just Kickin' It*," they both said in unison.

Marciana rewound the cassette tape until she reached the song. She turned the volume all the way up and took off her Walkman headphones and put them in between her and LaMonica so they could both hear the song.

They began singing the lyrics and snapping their fingers in harmony. "*Kick off your shoes and relax your feet. Just kickin' it, just kickin' it. Oh, yeah.*"

For LaMonica, the mind escape from problems didn't last long. The lyrics triggered her memory of a recent conversation with Bishop at home. They had a large stereo system Bishop had gotten from *somewhere* and on it was playing the *Just Kickin' It* song. LaMonica was singing along with the lyrics. Normally she only sang the hook part of the song because that's all most people knew. It was certainly all LaMonica had paid attention to.

In reality, the song was about being a so called "good woman" and taking care of your man. Bishop picked up on this right away as LaMonica was around the house singing the lyrics.

"Just kickin' it, just kickin' it. Me and my baby, yea."

Bishop blew his breath loudly and in an edgy tone of voice said, "Wait a minute, LaMonica. Did you hear that? That singer said, 'every man wants a woman that can cook him up a good meal'. Man, I did not know that song said that."

LaMonica picked up on his tone and decided she wasn't up for his challenge and attempted to walk from the living room into the dinning room. Bishop blocked her between the table and the bookshelf. He planted his legs in a wide stance and began waving his hands around in LaMonica's face.

"Hold up. Hold up. Did you know that?" Bishop asked with an edgy laughter. "Whoo hoo."

The house is neat, I'm off work and I'm in a good mood. I'm not going to let Bishop provoke me into being angry today, no matter how irritating he is. Ignoring him, LaMonica managed to maneuver around Bishop back to the living room. She frowned as she made it past him, rolling her eyes as she resumed singing, *"kick off your shoes and relax your feet -"*

Bishop cut her off. "Kick off yo' shoes and relax yo' feet! Say Whaaaat?" Bishop was getting increasingly snarky now.

"LaMonica, you've got to be kidding me. Are those words really coming out yo' mouth? Girl, you ain't even got the right to sang that song. And do you wanna know why?"

LaMonica didn't know how to answer Bishop when he got in these moods. One minute he would be calling her 'baby' and saying he'd do anything to protect her, and the next he would berate her for not taking care of him like he's her male child. She stood face to face with him with her tongue rubbing against the inside of her cheek, waiting for the reason she's not allowed to sing a song played on the radio. She already anticipated the answer would hurt.

Surely it would be another jab at how she just doesn't make the cut as a woman.

With a sour expression Bishop folded his arms across his chest and said, "Cuz you ain't even a real woman. That's why. You don't half cook around here. And you fa show don't know how to take care of a man like most women do. I could get any woman out here and she would be happy to cook and clean for me, run my bathwater, and even lay out my clothes."

What Bishop was saying stung. LaMonica had always tried to juggle all her responsibilities alongside with home. But if she was being honest with herself, she prioritized work, school, and Monica over everything. She rarely had much energy left over for anything else after that.

Bishop continued to look in LaMonica's direction, as if he expected some sort of response. She sucked her teeth and smacked her lips. It was the best response she could think of at the moment.

Bishop turning out to be so bad-tempered had blind-sided LaMonica. The ironic thing was that she had fled Mama's house and ran to him to escape the unhealthy feelings statements like these gave her from Ms. Demona and sometimes even Mama. But here Bishop was saying the same things, just in a different way.

LaMonica retreated into the bedroom to brush her hair while staring in the mirror. Truthfully, although she defended herself against the accusations of "not being good enough" deep down, she feared it was true. She just couldn't juggle everything. And why not? What was wrong with her? Why couldn't she be the "superwoman" that every Black woman was expected to be. Super at a career, super at being a mother of an obedient child, super at keeping an organized home.

The *Just Kickin' It* song ended and Marciana noticed LaMonica staring blankly off into space, deep in thought. She was no longer upbeat with the song. Her arms were hanging at her sides and Marciana was the only one still holding the Walkman headphone speakers.

"LaMonica, LaMonica."

LaMonica snapped out of her daze, realizing Marciana was calling her name.

"Hey, you checked out on me for a minute."

LaMonica's face was now expressionless. In a sad tone she said, "Yeah, that song just reminded me of an argument I had with Bishop."

"You guys are a family. Arguments come and go. That's normal. At least you're still together and raising your daughter."

"Yeah, I guess." LaMonica looked down while she thought about it.

"That's what I miss the most about my ex-fiancé, having a family. I really miss my stepdaughters."

"I didn't know you had a fiancé Marciana."

"Yeah, my mother and the rest of my family were all psyched to have a wedding. I was too, but things between us just didn't work out. I think my mom thinks it's my fault they didn't. She's been acting disappointed about it ever since."

"Awe dang I'm sorry."

"No, its fine being in a relationship like that was a learning experience. The next time I find true love I'm gonna hold on to my love." Marciana sang that last part in tune with the En Vogue song, "*Hold on to Your Love.*"

"Hahaha." She and LaMonica both laughed.

In an effort to keep both their moods pepped up, Marciana asked, "Hey which one of the Xscape singers do you like best?"

"I don't know. I don't really know them by name. Which-ever of the girls sings, *Who Can I Run To* is my favorite. That's a powerful song."

"Oh yes, you're right. I love that song too." Marciana began singing it, and just like that, both the girls' moods soared again.

Back in high school Marciana had made choices in dating that her mother didn't agree with (nothing to the degree of dilemmas that LaMonica presented Mrs. Powers with, but frustrations all the same). This caused their rela-tionship to become strained. Although out of respect she would rarely complain about her mother out loud, Marciana often felt slighted by the differences in her treat-ment of her verses her younger brother Mingo. Mingo was still at that young and cute stage. He could do no wrong and had not rubbed their mother's perfectionism the wrong way yet. The times Marciana had mentioned her mother's tone being so much nicer towards Mingo than her, LaMonica suspected the preferential treatment of a male in the family had more to do with Hispanic cultural norms than anything else. Marciana came from one of the most popular Mexican families in Saginaw. It had to be a good one, if she were to guess.

Despite the disappointment Marciana had brought her mother with her unconformity in proper dating etiquette, there was no doubt among anyone that she had made the right choices in high school extracurricular classes. Marciana had grown up singing in the choir at Arthur Hill High School and as a result she had developed her natural, raw, vocal abilities into a beautiful singing range that was pleasant to listen to.

Your choice in music can set the tone for the day, whether melancholy or upbeat. LaMonica and Marciana both went to school chipper that morning as Marciana happily sang entering the doors of PSI. Everything would change, however, when the administration staff came inside each of the classes for the big announcement that PSI was closing its doors.

2

ESCAPE

L aMonica and Marciana had very similar motives for attending computer school. They each just didn't know it. Marciana came from a well-known Mexican family in Saginaw. Her grandfather had built a six-figure business that produced the best corn tortillas this side of Mexico. Her mother had held a career in administration working for the city. It was incredibly important to Marciana that she make her family proud.

The expectations for LaMonica were a bit different. Mama had received a lot of flak from some of her family for adopting a half White child from a drug addicted prostitute. "That child ain't gonna turn out to be nothin'," the grandmother had often said. It was Mama's goal in life to prove them wrong.

Then there was Daddy. Daddy respected success and talent. Now that he was back in her life, she found herself to be on the descending end of his list of favorite children. His number one favorite had always been Malcolm. Malcolm had two things going for him. One—he was the baby and two—he could sing. Or sang as the old folks say. Malcom could really sang! When Nekeisha came along that knocked him out of the favorite for being the baby spot. Daddy had even given her a special nickname, Key Key, because she held the key to his heart. But Malcolm was still high on the list of importance because of his talent. Second in line if we're still counting.

Then there was Alvin. He was Daddy's second oldest child and had made it into the professional singing arena. This is where Daddy always wanted to be himself but didn't know how to go about it. Alvin had a singing contract with Atlantic records. When LaMonica met Alvin, she could tell despite his success he was still vying for Daddy's love and respect.

Chuck had the same mother as Malcolm, so they were a package deal. Plus, he could sing back up, so he was indeed high on Daddy's list. Brynner had the same mother as Alvin, and he at least understood music. But he was lower on the list than the other boys.

That just left Teddy, LaMonica and Ambrosia. The three of them had to get in wherever they could fit in, which for LaMonica was a tight squeeze. Teddy stayed to himself when it came to Daddy. LaMonica, Chuck, Malcolm and sometimes the other brothers would often go by and visit with him at his mother's house.

Ambrosia didn't care too much about Daddy's love and approval. She had her daddy in Detroit. It was more important to her to be close with Malcolm and Chuck than with their father. Daddy loved Ambrosia, but in some romanticized fantasy way of finally having his long-lost daughter back. If he had her right there in the city of Saginaw with him, she would likely be on the same descending end of the hierarchy of importance as LaMonica.

No, LaMonica seemed to be the only one **desperate** for

her father's love and approval. If Malcolm didn't invite her, she'd often hear about family get-togethers only *after* they'd happened. Or sometimes she would stumble upon them by stopping by Daddy's house, which he'd asked her to stop doing and to start calling first.

LaMonica had even remarked to Birdie that maybe she could earn Daddy's love and respect by being a successful computer operator. "He's going to be sorry that he ignored me when I'm doing well in computers someday." *I can't change the numbering of my birthing order and become the youngest. And I can't magically develop a talent for singing that I just don't have. But I can be the smartest and work towards having the most prominent career in the family someday.* Birdie had just listened, letting LaMonica vent. She knew that if LaMonica's goal didn't involve her ending up on the radio or the television set, it was an ill-fated plan. She just didn't have the heart to tell her at the time.

Marciana was 19, a year older than LaMonica. She was at an important crossroads in her life. She was on the verge of making a decision to live her life for herself and not for her mother or anyone else. *Maybe it's time I live my life for myself and see where that takes me,* she thought. Marciana's living situation was much more financially comfortable than LaMonica's because she lived at her mother's house. But Marciana was an organized long-term planner, and she had become increasingly frustrated with the amount of tuition PSI was charging. She calculated that she had racked up upwards of thousands of dollars in Federal Student Loans for a Data Entry certificate. She was weighing whether the cost had been justified to begin with.

Before leaving that day, the school had held a meeting and informed students that Jordan College (which was also in Flint) had made an agreement with the government to accept PSI students who hadn't finished their certificates. They were even willing to continue transporting the students by bus the first year.

That information was where the consistency in details ended. After the meeting LaMonica had spoken with her school counselor. He said if students took the transfer to Jordan College, they wouldn't owe the government all those thousands of dollars in loans they had racked up to obtain a simple certificate.

Marciana's counselor told her the very opposite. Her counselor said if she didn't transfer to Jordan College then she would no longer owe the government the outstanding loans because the school was being shut down. At the end of the day, LaMonica and Marciana grabbed two chairs from typing class and sat down in the hallway to compare notes.

Marciana appeared to be processing thoughts like a computer, as she was tapping her chin with her fingers.

"What are you doing, practicing 10-key typing, haha?" LaMonica asked.

"No, ha," Marciana answered in a playful tone before her words became more deliberate. "I'm counting up the costs. Do you realize we're going to have to pay these loans back that covered our tuition? And if we don't, we'll default with the government and won't be able to get any help in the future with school."

"Yeah Marciana, but that's only if what your counselor said was right. What if what my counselor said was correct?"

Marciana sighed. They were both more confused than ever. "What should we do then?"

"Hey look there's Mr. Black," LaMonica said. "I bet he'll know what's really up. Let's go ask him."

Mr. Black had been their favorite teacher because even though he taught the hardest class (Computer Programming), he offered them the most amusement. And anyone who could help LaMonica and Marciana get some laughs in was alright with them. Mr. Black was an odd-looking character, resembling an older version of the character Leroy from the 1980s hit show Fame. Sometimes he came in with his hair braided to the back and sometimes he just let it hang down on his neck.

"Doesn't it look like he's going to shake his leg and start singing beat it at any moment, haha?" Marciana had said in the middle of a test one day. LaMonica laughed so hard she was choking.

"Shhh. Here he comes."

"Yeah, here I come," Mr. Black said. Mr. Black's attempt at having a serious tone to reprimand his students always came off as if he was fighting hard to cover up a laugh within.

"Marcy, I think you should save your joke for LaMonica until after you're done with your test."

Oh shoot, Mr. Black had called Marciana "Marcy." LaMonica already knew what was coming next because if you ever wanted to see Marciana's chill mode go from 0 to 100, call her Marcy instead of Marciana. She'd go from happy-go-lucky to championship boxer fight mode before you could blink.

Here were the reasons behind it. First, she was named after her grandmother and that was extremely important to her. And second of all, Marcy was a socially acceptable whitewashed version of her true Latina name.

"Um, excuse me but my name isn't- she changed her tone to a more Caucasian sounding one, 'Marcy'."

Then she switched back into fight voice mode.

"It's Marciana."

You'd better believe she rolled that r hard and enunciated in perfect Spanish every vowel.

"If my mother would've wanted me named-" Caucasian tone again, 'Marcy,' - Latina fight mode again, "she would've named me that! I'm named after my grandmother, the beautiful Señora Marciana Guadalupe Jaramillo."

Oh Lord, have mercy, LaMonica thought. By this time, the entire class had paused to watch the exchange. Mr. Black's mouth had dropped, but you could still see he had found amusement in the situation. "My apologies, Marciana. Please save personal talk until after the test."

Marciana complied.

Whenever Mr. Black wasn't holding back chuckles from his students' antics, he was in serious teach mode. He was very passionate about teaching Computer Programming, even at its lowest level to Data Entry students. Whenever he could get his student's eyes to light up from knowledge, it made his day. Watching his class rotation of students go from complete bewilderment to writing computer prompts and commands were what excited Mr. Black.

LaMonica remembered that at the very beginning of classes last year he had said, "I know this all looks foreign to you now, but don't give up. As you keep taking what I'm saying and applying it one day, it'll just click and make sense." He was one of those teachers who really cared about his students attaining a new skill set. That's why it was so disheartening looking at him now, packing up his paperwork and belongings into a black soft leather crossbody bag and sighing, blowing his breath while probably wondering where he would work next.

"Mr. Black, can we talk to you for a minute?" Marciana began.

"Sure, guys what's up?" Mr. Black looked defeated as he stuffed more paperwork into the leather bag.

"Well, we're trying to figure out what to do. Should we take the offer to go to Jordan College or not? LaMonica's counselor told her to transfer, and my counselor advised me not to."

"Yeah, my counselor actually said if I don't transfer than that's what will make me liable for all these loans because I had an option to finish my education and didn't take it," LaMonica blurted out.

"You want my advice?"

"Yes," the girls said in agreement.

"My advice is to leave this place and don't look back. You've received a get out of jail free card to avoid these student loans. I'm still paying for student loans from college. Trust me, you don't want to be in that position." LaMonica glanced from Mr. Black and back to Marciana again. She was looking down and seemed to be in deep thought. No doubt what he said about student loans had grabbed her attention.

"Look, I'm not supposed to tell you this..."

LaMonica's eyes fixated intently on Mr. Black and what he was saying. It was a focus trick she used to retain information, especially when she felt a lot was coming at her at once.

"... but the government can't make you pay back those loans unless you transfer and finish out the program. My advice is to escape. Don't transfer. But you didn't hear it from me."

LaMonica was getting all As in her classes at PSI, something she'd never been able to do growing up in school. She felt pretty good about herself for that. Despite the fact that she was born with drugs in her system, despite the fact that

Angie's family wouldn't accept her because of her race, and most of all despite the fact that Ms. Demona and others had spoken curses over her life, she was still smart, and she could still accomplish something.

As she was walking out to the bus with Marciana, LaMonica's mind was racing through all the possibilities of her choices when it came to school. Owing back the student loan seemed to be a problem for down the road. One she didn't need to worry about right now, the way Marciana worried. Her primary concern was for the here and now. She had to worry about the needs and obstacles of today. And today she needed to be enrolled in somebody's school to keep her job and take care of herself and little Monica.

Just before they entered the yellow bus for home, a group of men in their 20s wearing white t-shirts approached them, selling M&M's. "Hey y'all help me free my brotha in jail."

"What'd he do?" LaMonica asked.

"He ain't do nothin.' They got my brotha sittin' in lock up on bull crap."

"I'll buy some M&M's to help out," Marciana said.

The boys eyed Marciana from head to toe. She just happened to be wearing name brand clothes that day and was sporting her fat gold chain.

"You look like you could buy this whole box of M&M's. Come on, quit playin' and help me free my brotha!"

Marciana pulled out $30 and bought the entire box of M&M's.

"That's what I'm talkin' about," the guy yelled. "Now all I got to do is find 10 more people like you and we got it."

Marciana was always doing stuff like that. She was kind-hearted sometimes to a fault. When they got on the bus, Marciana decided to just keep one individual package of the

M&M's candy. She and her mother were both supposed to be on a diet. They were taking special diet pills to lose weight and her mom would have a fit if she brought all that candy in the house.

"Here LaMonica, take this box home with you. My mom will lose it if I walk through the door with this much chocolate."

Marciana and LaMonica rode home, popping M&M's in their mouth and laughing about the good times they had at PSI, especially in Mr. Black's class. They both had a big decision ahead of them. In the end, they would choose different paths when it came to education. Each of their choices would help usher their destinies along.

3

LADIES' NIGHT

A s the girls talked on the bus ride home, they finally moved from *what to do about PSI* to more upbeat topics. Like the fact that LaMonica was preparing for her 18th birthday soon. Mama was planning her a cake and ice cream social. She invited Marciana to come, and she accepted.

"Hey girl, there's a Quinceañera coming up this weekend. Do you want to go with me?"

"Sure." LaMonica missed Quinceaneras and Mexican hall dances. She hadn't been to any with Luchie's family in a long time.

"I'm not sure what I'm wearing," Marciana said.

"Yeah, I don't know what to wear, either. I haven't gone out in a while."

"I'll tell you what, grab your going out clothes and I'll grab mine. I'll come pick you up early and we'll try each other's stuff on and see what we should wear."

"That sounds fun, but I have to warn you I don't have that much cute stuff."

"Girl, just come over. We're gonna look good, don't worry." They both laughed.

Now how am I going to get Bishop to agree to this? LaMonica thought.

Asking for permission to go to Marciana's house on Saturday wasn't that hard, since it was during the day. It was going to be Saturday night that would be the problem, and LaMonica knew it.

When Marciana and LaMonica pulled up at her house, her mother was home. She began yelling at Marciana from the kitchen, in a strong Spanish accent, right away.

"Why didn't you put the dishes away before you left this morning?"

"Ma, I was in a hurry. Couldn't Mingo put the dishes away since I did wash them?" Marciana answered her mother from the living room. Her mother still wasn't aware that company was in the house.

She whispered to LaMonica, "Watch her make an excuse for the golden child."

She made an excuse, but her tone had come down several octaves from passionately hot tempered to fervently warm. She began calling Marciana by her special name for her.

"Cianas, you know your brother has golf with your dad on Saturdays. Oh, hello who's this?"

"Ma, this is LaMonica (Lah moan ee ka)." Marciana said her name in a Spanish accent. LaMonica knew she had assumed she was at least part Mexican.

"Hello nice to meet you."

"Oh, she's pretty like you, mija. You should bring her to the dance tonight."

"I am Ma, that's why we have all these clothes to try on."

"Oh, I see now. You girls better make sure you pick all this stuff up when you're done."

"We will Mrs. Juarez."

"Oh, girl Juarez is my ex- husband's name. Call me Suela."

"Alright Suela."

"I can't wait for the dance tonight. I'm making fideo. Cianas, you're helping me too."

"Okay, Ma."

"LaMonica, make sure whatever you pick out is hot. You might catch you a husband at the dance tonight, girl. But if you do make sure you don't lose him like this one over here." Suela said this as she rolled her eyes in Marciana's direction and thumped her on the forehead while laughing.

"She already has someone, Ma."

"Oh well, back-up plan, eh? No, I'm just playing. I'm going to hit some rummage sales this morning. See you guys later."

"Man, your mom is doing like five things in one day."

"Girl, yeah, my mom stays active. It's those Pep a Trim diet pills I was telling you about." They both laughed.

"Diet pills are dangerous. You guys are on your own with those. I'm cool."

LaMonica looked around the house. Marciana had pictures upon pictures all over the walls, the end tables, under the end tables, everywhere. Her mother obviously had taken her to have quality pictures made throughout the years. LaMonica was such a visual person that all the neurons in her brain were firing off in excitement mode all at once.

"Oh my gosh, your pictures are so pretty. Especially your senior pics."

"Yeah, my mom got those for me."

Marciana's mother was obviously proud of her for graduating. She had senior pictures taken with outfit and background changes, as well as professional photos at an away location and inside the studio. LaMonica knew these were very expensive because she had worked as a temp answering phones at a professional photography studio.

"This one's, my favorite." Marciana pointed out a picture with an *In Living Color* 90s themed outfit. "We had my graduation event colors patterned after it."

Then Marciana pulled out some mementos from her graduation celebration. It was a full-on event her family had put on for her with an agenda program. On the back of the program were listed sponsors.

"What's this, sponsors?" LaMonica asked.

"This is how my family always does. Whenever somebody has an event, like a graduation or a Quinceañera or a wedding, we always have members of the family sign up to be sponsors and then we place their names on the back of the program to thank them."

Wow! Marciana comes from a really nice family, LaMonica thought.

Inside Marciana's room was a desk, where she pulled out a ton of invitations to upcoming family events. "Girl you should come with me to some of these."

"Man, you and your mom are always going somewhere."

"That's because I'm single. This is single Marciana. When I'm in a relationship, I'm just all about that person and I don't go anywhere or hardly do anything. I guess I'm getting it all out of my system before I find someone and get in a relationship again."

The girls mixed and matched clothing and accessories from each other's pile and finally dressed for the Quinceañera. Mama had little Monica for the weekend so the only issue for LaMonica was getting Bishop's approval. She started to call him, but didn't know what to say on the phone.

"Let me just go by my house and let my boyfriend know what I'm doing really quick."

"Okay."

Marciana lived on the South Side, so they quickly made it back to LaMonica's house on South Jefferson Street. Bishop was pleased to see her all dressed up.

"Oh, are we goin' out?" He asked with enthusiasm.

He had assumed that since LaMonica was dressed up; they were both going out together. She didn't know how to tell him otherwise, so she just put the clothing that she brought back from Marciana's in the bedroom. When she came back outside, Bishop had already spoken with Marciana and was climbing in the backseat.

"Hey before we head out, can you run me by the liquor store?"

"Yeah sure," Marciana said.

Marciana took Bishop to the liquor store. She and LaMonica both looked at each other. *I don't know what to do here,* LaMonica thought. Marciana saw it written all over LaMonica's face.

Bishop was back in a flash. Hey, run me by the weed man's house around the corner. Marciana took Bishop to the house he was requesting to go to. When he got back in the car, he seemed to be in an upbeat mood.

Marciana drove back to LaMonica's house.

"What are we doing here?" Bishop asked.

Marciana could see that LaMonica didn't know how to tell Bishop he wasn't invited, but she was up for the challenge. "Oh, tonight is girls' night, so it's just us ladies going out."

"Oh, straight uppppp? Oh okay. Okay." Bishop looked at LaMonica.

"Yep, just the girls," Marciana reiterated.

"Oh, I see. I got you. Okay. That's what we doin' now huh LaMonica? Alright, alright. Okay."

Bishop repeated himself multiple times as he was getting out of the car, looking at LaMonica all the while hinting with his eyes that she would pay for this later.

4

BIRDIE'S BACK

A ttending the Quinceañera had been fun. LaMonica's 18th birthday was fast approaching and like little Monica's birthday a few months back, LaMonica would spend yet another celebration with Mama at her house instead of home with Bishop.

Bishop hadn't "gotten her back" for going to the Quinceañera without him, but things hadn't gotten any better living with him on the South Side over on Jefferson Street. The roommate, Jessica, hadn't made any attempt to work, and Aunt Felisha was still there living upstairs, drug addicted, and stealing food from her refrigerator.

On the upside of things, Birdie had moved back to Saginaw with LaMonica's brothers, Malcolm, and Chuck. They would be attending her birthday social.

LaMonica had always spent a lot of time with Birdie as a child.

She was ecstatic that she had finally moved back to town. Ever since Mrs. Powers had allowed LaMonica to be around Birdie, Birdie had instructed LaMonica to call her "Mama."

"I'm yo' mama, not Mrs. Powers, not even Angie, but me. You and I always had a special connection. Ever since you were a little girl, like 2 or 3 years old, you would always find me. I remember one day I was at the laundry mat washing, and you just came up to me. I couldn't believe it. When I realized who you were, I shouted out 'Oh my goodness, this is my kids' sister.' I wish I could have gotten you, but Mrs. Powers had more pull with the courts and things like that than I did. But I'm yo' mama not her."

Birdie made these statements with such fervor throughout LaMonica's life that she thought she had to mean it with all her heart. She earnestly wanted Birdie to truly mean that word "Mama" like she did with her own sons, not only because of their closeness, but also because of the let downs she had experienced. She especially clung onto the belief that Birdie was a mother to her after her meeting with her bio mom and after that beat down Mama had given her.

What she wasn't prepared for was the way their dynamic would change since LaMonica had become a mother. Birdie commanded a lot of respect like Mama but in a more hood like way. Birdie and Mrs. Powers did not share the same values. As a matter of fact, Mrs. Powers had allowed LaMonica to be around Birdie as a child in a last resort compromise sort of way, as long as she still had control of the situation.

Now that LaMonica was becoming an adult, she was also realizing that a lot of the values Mama had taught her were important and she had adopted some additional ones of her own. Like for instance, she didn't want anyone smoking around little Monica. Not Bishop, not Birdie. Not anyone. This quickly became a problem because Birdie was a heavy smoker. She also had the same stance as Mama (as in no one should tell her what to do inside her own house).

Not only was Birdie's indoor smoking an issue for LaMonica, but her discipline methods as well. Birdie had always explained to LaMonica and her brothers that she had a hard life growing up. One where she didn't really get any toys to play with as a child. As a result, she collected toys in her adulthood. Now she didn't seem to make this analogy, but LaMonica had. All Birdie knew was these were her toys and her toys alone. And no one was to touch them unless she specifically gave permission for them to do so. There were toys hanging up next to pictures all over the walls (pictures were her second love). Toys were on end tables and shelves all over the living room. There were toys sitting neatly on top of her dressers and nightstands in her bedroom. She even had bookshelves with not books but— you guessed it toys, toys, toys.

Birdie had an enormous collection of Furbies, Holiday and Special Edition Barbies, Marvel action figures. A Hot Wheel collection and every new Happy Meal toy promotion McDonald's had come out with for the last 10 years.

This toy house was a dream for any child to walk into and at age one and a half, little Monica couldn't resist running towards all the bright and beautiful toys to grab one.

"Uh uh. You'd better quit or I'm gonna pop you," Birdie had shouted out the first time LaMonica had brought her over.

LaMonica's mouth fell open, and her eyes blinked slowly toward Birdie. *Is she really going to pop my daughter?*

Little Monica only halted for a moment and then the bright toys began calling to her again and she grabbed one.

"Uh oh, that's it. You dun done it now. Let me get my

stick." Birdie yelled this out as if it were a command, but there was a hint of playfulness in her voice—which LaMonica did not catch. The only thing LaMonica was focused on was the fact that now Birdie had retrieved a ruler and was tapping it against the inside of her hand while walking towards little Monica.

"You'd better put it down or I'm gonna pop you one."

Startled, little Monica dropped the toy and ran crying to her mother.

"Don't go cryin' to yo' mama. Come over here and put my toy back in its place unless you want me to pop you."

That's when LaMonica spoke up. "No, you're not going to hit my child with a ruler."

"Don't say that in front of her. I'm not really gonna hurt her."

Birdie had given little Monica a nickname, "Moni." That was just part of Birdie's personality. She was always renaming other people's kids. And they for doggone sure had better answer to their new nickname. Her personality was forceful. This was implied. Little Monica had learned right away that her new nickname was Moni, and that Birdie was to be obeyed.

"Moni, go in there in the bedroom and watch cartoons on my TV while I talk with yo' mama." Little Monica quickly obeyed.

She motioned to LaMonica. "Come on, let's sit in the kitchen at the table where we can talk."

"LaMonica," Birdie enunciated LaMonica's name as if she was really trying to get some information to her and have her see things from her side.

"You have to be careful what you say around them (them being children). I wasn't going to hit her for real. I was just trying to scare her. That's how you train them. Now if you didn't like what I was doing, you should have waited until everything was over and told me in private. Not in front of her."

"Okay, but I thought you were going to hit my child with a ruler, and I wasn't just going to stand there."

"Nooo. Couldn't you tell by my voice, the way I was sayin' it, that I was just trying to scare her?"

"I didn't know what was going on, but I don't agree with that either anyway."

While LaMonica was pregnant, attending classes as a teen at Ruben Daniels, they had taught them parenting lessons. She learned that even small children should have boundaries, but they should be reasonable. LaMonica didn't feel that a child maintaining self-control in a room full of toys was reasonable.

"What child isn't going to want to touch and play with a room full of toys? They taught me at school if there's anything you don't want the child to touch, you should put it up high out of reaching distance. Any child would have done what little Monica did today."

"No, that's not true. A lot of family stops by here and I have all the children trained not to touch any toy in here, unless I give them my permission. And most of the time I don't have to pop them. I just threaten to do it and they stop. And if I have to take and pop one, I grab some newspaper or something that doesn't hurt to do it. It's just scaring them, not really hurting them. Don't you see that LaMonica? I'm training them."

"Do you mean the way you train your dogs with newspaper?" LaMonica had watched Birdie train puppies and dogs for years. She was the best at it. But this wasn't exactly the kind of training she had in mind for little Monica. Not that she exactly knew what she was doing when it came to disciplining a child either, but she just knew she didn't agree with this.

Birdie sensed that between LaMonica's tone and her stance, she would not be able to sway her over to her side of thinking and she wasn't used to that. People usually agreed with Birdie and did what Birdie said simply because it was her and because of her commanding street demeanor. Anything outside of compliance would be seen as disrespect, something Daddy's other kids would never do. This angered and frustrated Birdie to the point that she pronounced her first curse over little Monica.

"Well, I'll tell you what, if you don't get that girl to be obedient by the time she's 5 years old, you can hang it up. It'll be too late, and she'll be out of control. That's what I always say, 'train them up by the time they're 5 or it's too late'."

"But I'm done going back and forth with you on that. You'll see at some point. Here, let me make you a sandwich. Do you want a tomato on yours?"

"Sure."

Birdie had gotten up from the table and was sauntering around the kitchen, wiping and straitening areas as she made her and LaMonica and little Monica sandwiches.

"Man, you know what's crazy? I'll tell you what's crazy is how there's some uppity Black people who shouldn't even be considered Black. They run around here actin' and talking White. Hell, I'm blacker than those women, with their uppity selves."

LaMonica wasn't sure of who these "other Black people" Birdie was speaking of were, but she found it odd that Birdie, being a Caucasian woman, was saying that some Black people weren't Black if they were "uppity." Of course, Birdie would never categorize herself as a Caucasian because she was part Mexican, and that's what she embraced the most.

It became clear to LaMonica that Birdie's definition of "Black" meant that a person had to embrace the stereotypes that were put upon Blacks and had to have a culturally accepted monolithic thought pattern in order to be "truly Black enough" to be considered Black despite genetics or skin tone. This is why Birdie felt comfortable placing herself in that category, because she happily embodied most stereotypes given to African Americans.

LaMonica left Birdie's house that day with a lot of bad feelings. But she and Birdie were family and family often hurt each other and moved on like nothing happened. Or so LaMonica thought. She would later find out that her descent would not be so easily forgiven or forgotten by Birdie.

5

PRETTY HAIR GANG

The day of LaMonica's 18th birthday celebration at Mama's house didn't look much varied from little Monica's 1st birthday party a few months ago. All it was missing was a Pin the Tail on the Donkey game. Mama had set up streamers and balloons outside on the stairs just like they did for Monica's birthday.

Between all the streamers and balloons, Monica was full of excitement at the idea of another birthday party. At just 14 months old, her vocabulary was quite good for a toddler. She was jumping all over the place, throwing streamers and playing balloon toss with her grandmother and mother.

"Mama, we're having a birthday, yay!"

"Yes baby. My friend Marciana is coming over and your uncles are coming too."

"Yay. Mama, am I going to the party too?"

"Yes, baby, it's going to be here. You'll be here too."

"Thank you." Birdie had taught her to say, 'please' and 'thank you' and she now used them in her vocabulary as often as she could.

Mama had borrowed a friend's car and they all road over

to Birdie's house and picked up Malcolm and Chuck for the party.

"Mama said make sure you stop in when you come back because she wants to see you for your birthday," Chuck said.

"Alright, I will," LaMonica replied.

"Are there gonna be any chicks at this party?" 15-year-old Malcolm asked.

"Uh, you're way too young for my friends Malcolm."

"Aye, don't tell nobody my age. I'm tryin' to get me a 'Sallie'." Malcolm said.

"Yeah, don't tell nobody my age either, Hattie." Chuck chimed in.

Chuck and Malcolm had their own sort of language they had learned from Daddy. Often men were called "Herman" and women had a few names to describe them, "Sallie," "Hattie," and "Pet."

Birdie had once told LaMonica that Daddy and his family developed this lingo to hide when they were talking about someone in the presence of others. For instance, one could simply replace the name of a female in the room with "Pet" or replace the name of someone who was known to others in the room and the gossip they were speaking wouldn't be understood.

The male members of the family had developed this language to have a deeper meaning, however. "Sallie" generally meant a girl they wanted to have some sort of relations with. It was even used to describe genitalia at times. "Hattie" was usually a cool female and if someone was called "Pet" (which was a country way of saying Pat), there was generally something wrong with them.

Chuck and Malcolm were very handsome when placed in any category. But they were especially appealing to both teen girls and women in the hood because light skinned boys were always in season.

DNA is a funny thing; it mixes from each side differently in some. In Malcolm's case, he had taken on more of his mother's complexion and hair, yet somehow had Daddy's eyes and nose. This made him appear to be a Hispanic with Black swag. Chuck looked like a light-skinned, young, Black man. He had hair that could be tamed and waved with products or curly and afro'd out without.

At just 15 and 16, they both appeared older than they really were. LaMonica agreed to keep their secret, and they arrived at the big yellow house on 5th street for the party.

At LaMonica's birthday celebration, there was no drinking of alcohol, just cake, ice cream, and music videos. Mama had ordered pizza like back when she had a birthday party once in junior high. When Marciana arrived, it bewildered her how childlike LaMonica's birthday was. She looked at Chuck and Malcolm to see if they were as surprised as she was. That's when Marciana and Chuck's eyes locked.

Chuck and Marciana found a quiet corner of the house to slip off to. They seemed to hit it off right away. Whenever LaMonica and Malcolm weren't trying to do the latest dance move from a music video or cracking jokes, she'd look over at them and they were fully engrossed in each other. Chuck was telling her some sort of warm-hearted story (probably about one of his pit bull puppies) because Marciana kept putting her hand over her heart and saying, "awe." They were both leaning forward, sitting angled towards one another, and had forgotten anyone else was in the room.

As expected, Chuck lied and told 19-year-old Marciana he was an adult like her. LaMonica kept her word and didn't get involved not wanting to mess up his "game."

Besides, this was just one fun evening, right? It's not like Marciana and Chuck were going to become an item or something.

Chuck and Malcolm both had beautiful singing voices like Daddy, and so they sang along with some of the more popular R&B songs. That did it for Marciana: she completely swooned over Chuck after that. After the same R&B songs had cycled through on the television, Marciana became visibly bored with LaMonica's juvenile birthday party. Even Chuck and Malcolm were used to more adult partying than this. So, when Marciana announced "let's head out and party for real" everyone was ready to change up the pace. Mama agreed to watch little Monica, and everyone headed out in the late model silver sedan Marciana had borrowed from her mom.

Not only were Chuck and Malcolm handsome but they were what the hood called "pretty boys." Having nice hair, clothes, and even a manicure, in Chuck's case, was very important to them, just like their dad.

The "pretty boys" even had a beauty routine. They believed in tying their hair up at night, so they looked well-groomed during the day. They didn't stray from that routine for anything. And tonight was no different. Chuck had on a white bandana tied around his head to keep his soft curls neat and Malcolm had a blue bandana tied around his silky hair. Blue bandanas were usually looked at as a gang sign, but Malcolm didn't seem to care. He must have just grabbed whatever color bandana was available without giving it much thought.

Marciana drove everyone around to the same spots everyone else rode to on the East Side of Saginaw on a weekend night. First down East Genesee Street. Then a stop and park at the 7-11 to see who was chilling up there. But not for too long because gang enemies often confronted each other there with gunfire.

Chuck rode in the front with Marciana. She ran her palm over his sleeve and squeezed his forearm. "Where should we go?"

Chuck appeared to be in a trance, staring at Marciana's lips. LaMonica and Malcolm were in the backseat cracking jokes about the whole thing. Since Chuck was in a daze, Malcolm was happy to answer. He was ready for something strong to drink, as usual.

"Hey if you head up to the liquor store on Remington, we can grab some dranks. They let me buy there."

Marciana headed down Hess Street and back up Remington towards the store for alcohol. That's when the police got in behind them.

"Oh Sh*#! They're pulling me over," Marciana exclaimed.

LaMonica looked back at the police car and lights.

"Don't look back. You ain't never supposed to look back at the police," Malcolm said.

"Well, does everybody have their seatbelts on?" LaMonica asked nervously.

"Cuz I don't have mine on. Should I put it on?" She continued.

"No, don't make no sudden movements, Hattie," Chuck said.

"Besides, you don't have to wear a seat belt in the backseat anyways."

Malcolm put his hands out as if he was patting the air sideways. "Y'all just be cool!"

Malcolm and Chuck had already been taught that a respectful attitude to authority goes a long way. After straightening themselves and clearing their throats, they were nervous, but prepared for the officers to approach.

Two officers approached the car, a White one and a Black one. They were both holding flashlights. The Black officer was shining the flashlight in the car while his partner spoke with Marciana.

Being stopped by the police put most people from the hood on edge. Some were doing something wrong; some weren't. While the officer was asking Marciana for her license and registration, LaMonica searched hard in her mind. *Are we breaking any laws I haven't thought about? I don't think so.*

"What gang are you in?" the officer asked Malcolm.

"Gang?" Malcolm was perplexed.

"Yeah gang. You're both wearing head rags. You in particular have on blue, so what set you claiming, young brother?"

Malcolm laughed. "I ain't claiming no set, sir. Hahaha."

"I'm serious," the officer continued. "There's a lot of gang activity that goes on out here. Now you're wearing that blue rag, what gang are you all in."

"Sir, this is called the keepin' your hair together gang." Malcom smiled to show the officer his sincerity while patting his hair.

LaMonica cocked her head to the side and reached over Malcolm. "Sir, my brother's not in a gang. He just moved here. He just likes being cute that's all."

"Well, you need to be careful about putting those rags on your head. That's considered gang paraphernalia around here. There's been so many shootings that when we see that we're going to automatically assume you're in a gang. Especially in this part of town."

"Okay, sir. I'll get me some different colors cuz I gotta keep the head right." Malcolm giggled.

"I need to see everyone in the car's ID," the other officer announced.

LaMonica showed the officer her ID.

"You just made the 18 mark today, huh?"

"Yes. Yes, sir." LaMonica responded.

In a slow rhythmic way (with a bit of attitude) Marciana explained, "That's... why... we're... out celebrating tonight... because it's her birthday."

"And what about you fellas where's your IDs?"

"I don't have an ID," Chuck explained.

"Yeah, me neither." Malcolm added.

"Why don't you have IDs?" The officer asked.

"I mean, I've never needed one," Chuck answered.

"How old are you?" the police officer asked, catching on that Chuck was underage.

"16," Chuck answered. Marciana's eyes bucked at him.

"And what about you?" the officer asked Malcolm.

"I'm 15."

"Marciana Juarez, you have minors in your car. It is well past curfew for these minors to be out without a parent. You do understand that as the driver you are responsible if anything happens to them."

"Yes, sir." Marciana's attitude was much more compliant now that she knew she had minors in the car after hours.

Chuck was thoroughly embarrassed. He seemed to freeze in place and swallow the air hard.

"Okay, I'm gonna let you guys go with a warning. No drinking and get those minors home."

"Okay, I will officer." Marciana said.

"I'm serious. If I see you all out here again tonight, I'm not going to be so nice."

"Well, I guess I'd better get everybody home."

Chuck directed Marciana to Birdie's house. When they

pulled up in the driveway, Chuck turned to LaMonica, "Don't forget Mama wants you to come in."

"Okay Chuck. Come in Marciana and I'll introduce you."

Once inside, Birdie hugged LaMonica.

"Happy birthday. I love you."

"I love you too."

"This is my friend Marciana from computer school. Marciana, this is Chuck and Malcolm's mother, Birdie."

"Chuck and Malcolm's mother? Well, ain't I your mother too?"

"Yeah, Mama."

"Well then, don't be comin' in her talkin' about no Birdie. Now my daughter wants to call me by my name now, I see."

LaMonica blew her breath.

"Don't be blowin' your breath at me or you might not get your birthday present." Birdie said this playfully.

"Come in the room, I've got something special for you."

In her bedroom, Birdie pulled out a ring. "This ring is special to me. It's the only thing I have left of my mother, and I want you to have it, because you truly are my daughter."

LaMonica couldn't believe Birdie would give her something so precious. They embraced.

"Te amo," Birdie said.

"Te amo," LaMonica replied.

When LaMonica and Birdie came back into the living room, Malcolm had grabbed a beer and retreated upstairs to sing loudly along with his stereo and to let Chuck and Marciana have some alone time. They were cuddled up on the sofa in an embrace and kissing. Birdie cleared her throat, and they both jumped back. LaMonica and Birdie both laughed.

"Make sure you call me tonight," Chuck said, never taking his eyes off Marciana.

"Oh, I will," Marciana said flirtatiously.

"Ummm," LaMonica said, smiling at Birdie

They both laughed.

6

HER OWN PATH

The next day Marciana stopped by Birdie's house and began spending time with Chuck. Chuck was still in high school, so he didn't have money for dates. Most of him and Marciana's time was spent in his room or watching movies at his house (Birdie had an extensive collection of those too). Birdie didn't have a car, so Marciana would give her rides in her mom's car to wherever she needed to go during the day. Through this, they became close.

Once Marciana came to visit Chuck after LaMonica's birthday, she and Chuck were a couple from that day forward. She was always at Birdie's house. Marciana spent so much time there, it frustrated her mother to the point of asking her to move out. Soon Marciana was living in Birdie's house with Chuck.

LaMonica went to visit Marciana at Birdie's house after a couple of weeks, and she was completely immersed in being a part of her new family.

"Oh, hey Hattie," Marciana greeted her with cheer while carrying a basket of laundry.

"Hey Hattie," LaMonica greeted her back with laughter. *Wow, so Marciana has picked up on the language quickly.*

"I have a ride to the water park do you want to come?"

"No, I'm just gonna stay here with Chuck today. I have to finish washing clothes and then cook him some dinner. Besides, I have an appointment coming up. What time is my appointment Mama?"

Marciana was now calling Birdie Mama.

"I think it's not until 1pm."

"We have a surprise for you. You're going to be an auntie," Marciana said.

"Yep, it's true at 16 your brother is preparing to become a father," Birdie added.

"Oh, wow congratulations," LaMonica said.

"Well, listen, you could leave Moni here while you go to the water park," Birdie suggested.

"Oh, thanks, but I'm actually taking her with me. I just have to go pick her up from my mom."

"Oh, so she's with Mrs. Powers?" Birdie said this in a frustrated tone because she'd asked LaMonica for Moni several times and LaMonica had often told her no.

"I've gotta run. Talk to you guys later."

"Bye Hattie," Marciana said as LaMonica was leaving.

"Bye Hattie," LaMonica replied.

As soon as LaMonica was gone, Birdie vented to Marciana. "Man, I can't ever get my granddaughter. Every time I ask LaMonica to get Moni she turns me down."

"Don't worry Mama, when I have this baby you can keep it whenever you want to."

"Thank you mija."

Marciana was already turning into "Relationship Marciana." She differed greatly from "Single Marciana."

Relationships were changing all around LaMonica.

Once Marciana moved in with Birdie, she quickly became like a daughter to her. Her favorite daughter. That used to be LaMonica's position. She and Birdie used to talk, read stories together, watch shows and laugh and enjoy each other's company for hours on end. Especially when she was younger, and Birdie lived in Saginaw.

Things changed subtly between LaMonica and Birdie from the moment Chuck met Marciana. LaMonica had hardly noticed it at first. When she finally did, it was so glaring that it was blinding.

Birdie came from a background of rejection like LaMonica did. Both her Caucasian and Hispanic side of the family had done this to her. But it was most important for her to receive approval from the Hispanic side. Chuck had presented Marciana as a solution to this problem.

"Mama, now that I have a Mexican girlfriend and we're going to have a Mexican baby maybe your dad will talk to you."

Birdie dismissed it as the sweet hopes of a teenage son. But unconsciously she latched onto this concept all the same. It would eventually play out in her division of treatment between Marciana and LaMonica. She was, after all, having her REAL grandbaby.

Being in Birdie's good graces once upon a time had felt good. A sense of belonging to someone who looked more like her than Mama. Someone who was younger, prettier, cooler even, and wanted to be her parent. Sadly, LaMonica would endlessly seek this woman's approval out of desperation for eons.

LaMonica's relationship with Birdie wasn't the only one that was changing. Even though she still lived with Bishop, she no longer looked at him the same way. She couldn't quite place her finger on it, but something was very different between them. If he even tried to touch her in bed, she felt a sickening feeling inside.

"Baby, it's that thang in your arm. The Norplant. It's the hormones that are making you this way." Bishop would say.

Deep down LaMonica knew it wasn't just the hormones. She had finally had her fill of Bishop Holmes. She only felt dread now that she was stuck with him. At times his "sweet talk" in the bedroom was to get on top of her and say, "If you ever leave me, I'll kill you. You hear me. I'll kill you if you ever leave."

Somehow Bishop thought this was sexy. LaMonica was stuck. She had a baby with him, and she was just stuck.

From as far back as LaMonica could piece it together, her nauseous reaction to Bishop's advances began when she watched him ignore the financial responsibilities of taking care of their daughter time and time again. LaMonica was constantly broke meanwhile Bishop seemed to live carefree and duty free.

Now that she was 18, LaMonica no longer qualified for a dependent Social Security check from Mama. Technically, she now received her full Aid to Dependent Families and Children (AFDC) government check. Over 90% of it went to pay the rent, however. The government check was set up on what was called a vendor pay schedule. It went straight from the State of Michigan Treasury to the vendor, a.k.a. the land-lord. They mailed her out a check for the remaining balance of $18 every two weeks. She usually used this for gas money to catch rides to buy groceries.

Obviously, this wasn't enough to take care of Monica's needs, not to mention the electric and power bill. No, she had to accomplish all of this alone using her part-time stipend she received through the JTPA program for working in the Prosecuting Attorney's Office for Child Support.

Working there had become an eye opener as well. LaMonica saw first-hand what a child having a responsible father looked like. Oh sure, fathers often came in denying the paternity of the child in question because of the circumstances. But once that DNA test came back positive, they weren't too reluctant to go ahead and set up child support payments through their job.

Now of course there were still some fathers who didn't agree with the amount or even some who tried to evade child support all together. In those cases, the court would petition to have their wages garnished and the child would be taken care of. LaMonica knew she would never have any recourse like that because Bishop purposely didn't work and refused to be a productive member of society.

After the last day of school at PSI, LaMonica knew she had the spring and summer to figure something out. The JTPA counselors would be looking for a fall school schedule for her to continue her assignment at the courthouse. She was already skating on thin ice because she had turned 18 (which is when JTPA assignments typically ended) and somehow; they hadn't noticed. The office manager Susan in the Prosecuting Attorney's Office for Child Support had noticed, however.

"Hey, I know you just had your birthday and turned 18. When the interns turn 18 the assignments usually end but they haven't mentioned it over at the JTPA office and so I won't mention it either. Make sure you don't mention it either."

"I won't." LaMonica agreed.

Susan really liked LaMonica. The Prosecuting Attorney's Office for Child Support was a small and diverse office. There were two attorneys, three clerks, and an office manager. Each quarter they rotated having two new interns.

LaMonica had been there the longest because Susan was so fond of her.

The three clerks were all women of color. One was Mexican and two were Black.

One day one of them remarked, "Hmm Susan's kept you around longer than that White girl intern we once had. She must really like you."

Susan did really like LaMonica and so did the attorneys in the office. They knew LaMonica was working on borrowed time because if anyone at the JTPA program realized she was now 18 she would lose the position.

Susan got LaMonica an interview to work in one of the judge's offices at the courthouse. She also gave her a glowing recommendation letter. LaMonica was required to take a test to work in the Clerk's office and she passed, but even with Susan's recommendation the hiring manager couldn't get over the fact that LaMonica didn't have a high school diploma or a G.E.D. so she didn't get the job.

Everyone was so disappointed because they knew LaMonica would eventually have to leave, and they wanted her to still work closely with them by clerking for the judge. That's when LaMonica realized how important a G.E.D. was. Even with secretarial and data entry training, she still needed it. LaMonica liked to jump over steps when she could, but this was one she knew she would have to face sometime soon if she ever wanted a better job in life.

LaMonica continued to work at the courthouse over the spring and summer and thankfully no one who mattered to her lively hood noticed she had turned 18.

Somehow, she managed to scrape by financially, as Monica was getting bigger and growing in shoe and clothing sizes. After taking care of the household bills and Monica's needs, there wasn't any money left over for anything else.

Meanwhile, Bishop was living his life carefree, drinking, and hanging out with his friends. As a result, LaMonica's level of respect for him was at an all-time low. As the respect was leaving the romantic love was swiftly following.

Oh, she still loved him, but in that *I hope nothing bad ever happens to you kind of way.* Not in a desirable way, like when they first met.

∾

*N*ear the end of summer, Jordan College and the Federal Student Loan program reached out to LaMonica. The Federal Student Loan agent urged her to attend Jordan College.

"I was told I wouldn't owe the student loan if I didn't transfer because the government shut the school down."

"Well, I don't know who told you that, honey, but they've given you some wrong information. If you don't transfer to the college, we're making available to you, you will still owe the loan because we made a way for you to continue your certificate program."

"So, you're saying either way I'm responsible for the loan, whether I return to school or don't?"

"Yes. That's what my understanding is," the agent said.

Honestly, no one seemed to be really sure.

LaMonica consulted Marciana on what she was going to do. Now that she was living with Chuck and pregnant, she had no plans to return to school. And was still of the firm belief that not transferring would save her from having to pay the ridiculous loan back for a certificate.

Bishop and Alonzo had abandoned the program long ago and now even Marciana. LaMonica decided she would continue her path on stepping out on her own when it came to education. She decided she would go for it. She would attend Jordan College.

Jordan College set up transportation at the downtown mall for all the PSI students that would be continuing. And LaMonica started up her old routine again- school, work, and take care of Monica.

7

MR. SWAY

On day one, Jordan College was very different from PSI. It was a REAL college. They had a basketball team and a step team. They had a school newspaper and all sorts of activities to get involved in.

They even had a cafeteria. That's where she met HIM. In the cafeteria. She would later learn his name was Coby Sway. She didn't pay him much attention at first, other than he was a nice-looking guy. Obviously, a jock on the basketball team. Easily identifiable as upper middle class born and bred. He probably knew nothing about what it was like to struggle in the hood. LaMonica usually didn't even allow herself to look at dudes like him. What would one want with her?

That's why it was such a surprise to her when he sent his wing man over (which LaMonica had never seen played out in action before).

"Hey. Do you see my friend over there?"

"Yeah," LaMonica responded.

"Well, he likes you and he wants to know if he can have your name and phone number."

"Maybe I don't believe you."

"No seriously, he told me to come over here and ask you this."

LaMonica had never really seen this wing man routine played out before. It sort of baffled her. In her mind she was questioning whether the guy who was talking to her was the one that actually wanted this information or was it his tall friend?

A professional voice mixed with a hood attitude rose up from LaMonica.

"Well, if he wants all that information, he's going to have to ask me himself. He can't send someone over here to do it for him like a little boy."

LaMonica watched as the basketball player walked across the room to relay her message to his teammate.

She looked this interested fellow over thoroughly this time. *Maybe I should take notice of him.* He was tall, very tall. He had wavy hair and high cheekbones. To top it off, he was incredibly handsome. This guy's looks were the stuff romance novel covers were made of. You could tell he had well-developed chest muscles even while he was wearing his shirt. He was attractive and not hood. His clothes were well fitted and didn't hang off him like some gangster.

Only thugs ever tried to holler at her, because that's where she came from, where thugs reside. No, this guy was different. He was her fantasy guy. This was unreal.

LaMonica watched Coby get ready to come over. He nodded to the information his friend gave him, straightened himself, nodded again, and walked towards her.

When he reached her with confidence he said, "Hi I'm Coby Sway. Can I get your name?"

"LaMonica (La moan eka)," she enunciated with a strong Spanish accent.

"Oh, that's unique. Is that Spanish?"

"Yes." LaMonica lied.

"I'm part Cherokee Indian, myself."

"Yeah, I can kind of tell. Is that why your hair is like that?" Coby's hair was tall and wavy.

"I guess so. I get it from my grandma."

He was even hotter up close. LaMonica studied his face and his lips as he spoke. Coby had a natural red rouge to his cheeks.

Coby rubbed the back of his head and said, "I'm on the basketball team. I would really love for you to come out to some of my games."

"I figured you were on the basketball team because of your height. How tall are you?"

"6'4," Coby replied.

Wow, the difference in their height was stark. LaMonica was just barely over five feet tall.

"So will you come to my next game?"

"I'd really like to, but I live in Saginaw, and I don't really have a ride to get here after school, sorry."

"Saginaw. Oh, is that where all those students are coming from on the bus in the morning?"

"Yes."

"How far away is Saginaw?"

"You're not from around here, are you?"

"No, actually I'm from Springfield, Illinois."

"How did you end up here?" Jordan college wasn't that well known. Even though it was a four-year university, most of its students came from the surrounding communities.

"The basketball coach recruited most of the players on the team from Illinois. When I was in high school, I played basketball, and scouts and coaches would often come and watch me play. Jordan College had a good offer so here I am."

Yes. Here you are! LaMonica thought.

Summer, who rode the bus from Saginaw with LaMonica, hollered out. "Hey y'all better wrap it up. You don't want to be late for class."

"I've got to head out to class. It was nice meeting you, Coby."

"Hey, listen, can I have your phone number? I'd love for us to talk more."

Usually in these situations LaMonica would be cute and give a fake phone number. Heck, usually in these situations she didn't have this much conversation with a guy who was interested in her. But to her own surprise, she heard herself spouting out Mama's number to Coby as if it were her own.

"Okay, I'm gonna call you after practice later."

"Wait! About what time would that be?"

"Probably around 8:30 tonight." He smiled and ran off to practice.

I'll have to stay at Mama's house late tonight to catch his call, LaMonica thought.

LaMonica stayed as late as she could at Mama's house after school. She arranged for a friend to give her a ride home at 9pm. Coby called, and they had about 30 minutes to talk.

Coby led most of the conversation, which she was grateful for. Dating or talking to guys outside of Bishop just wasn't something she was used to, and LaMonica found herself being surprisingly shy on the phone with Coby.

The next day at school, they ate lunch together at the cafeteria. She began to get more and more comfortable with him. He introduced her to his basketball friends and their girlfriends. Some attended the nearby satellite college of the University of Michigan—U of M of Flint.

LaMonica had never been friends with college people before. Their whole conversation was elevated. They were all going for bachelor's degrees at prestigious colleges. They discussed financial planning and, of course, regular womanly topics.

Most of the time, when Coby called Mama's house, LaMonica wasn't "home" because she was at her real house with Bishop. Mama was starting to apply the pressure to her.

"LaMonica, you need to tell that boy the truth instead of having him callin' here thinking you live here."

The look LaMonica gave Mama told her she wasn't planning on following her advice.

"Okay. Well, I'll tell you one thang, the next time that boy calls here I'm gonna tell him, 'LaMonica doesn't live here. She's at her own house'."

"Mama." LaMonica whined and blew her breath.

"You're the one that's always telling me I'm not married to nobody, and I don't owe Bishop nothin'."

"And that's true. But you shouldn't be playin' with that college boy like that LaMonica. That's how folks get hurt."

LaMonica had to think fast. She couldn't keep staying late at Mama's house to catch Coby's phone calls, and she couldn't keep being always "not home" when he called either. So, she decided the best way to head off Mama saying the wrong thing to Coby on the phone was to start calling him instead. She began calling him whenever Bishop was away from the house in the evenings. She would just make an excuse that Monica needed her whenever Bishop was coming in the door.

Coby was very trusting. He never suspected anything.

Besides, he was too busy being productive to have time to calculate LaMonica's moves. Between school, homework, and basketball practice, Coby's schedule was full.

They continued having lunches together at school and getting to know one another better. Eventually, he wanted to come and visit her at her home. LaMonica agreed.

"Mama, Coby wants to come and visit me."

"Here?" Mama pointed at the floor as if to ask *in this house*?

"Yes, Mama here. Can he come?"

"I guess LaMonica. I hope you know what you're doin'."

"Okay, Mama."

LaMonica's friend Jacqueline, who lived around the corner from Mama, had started seeing an older guy named Big Jimmy. Ironically enough, Big Jimmy's father was a security guard for the same company as Mrs. Powers. Both he and his father knew Mrs. Powers well and had known LaMonica since she was a little girl.

LaMonica set up a ride home from Big Jimmy for that Friday evening. She told Bishop she had to go to Mama's house to wash clothes (which was true) and everything was all set.

Coby didn't have a car, so his teammate brought him to Saginaw to visit. When he arrived, he had two individual roses, one for Mama and one for LaMonica.

Mama was grinning from ear to ear. Between his tall, handsome looks and that rose, Coby had won her over rather quickly.

Mama took little Monica into the room for bed with her so LaMonica could visit in private with Coby. He held her right hand in his and kept flexing his watch with his left hand.

Coby wore a Rolex, but LaMonica was oblivious to this

because details weren't her thing. Finally, after so much flexing and LaMonica not noticing his treasure, he finally came out and talked about it.

"You know I respect you for being a single mother. My mother had to raise us by herself after my father deserted her. They were married for years and then he left my beautiful mother with six children for a younger woman.

"My father is an engineer and highly paid, but he left her with nothing. And my mother is so sweet she wouldn't even pressure him for child support. We went from living in the suburbs to living in the poorest part of the city.

"At times when my mother was struggling to pay bills and juggling bill money with food money, she would call my dad and ask for help. And do you know what he would tell her?"

"What?" LaMonica intently asked.

"He would tell her no, and that if she can't afford to raise us without help, then she should give us to him."

"I still love my father and fight to respect him because Jehovah says we are to respect our parents, but it's hard after watching how he treats my mother.

"When I went off to college, my dad was proud of me, but he thought I could have done better. Picked a more prestigious school to play ball at and have a better opportunity to get picked by the NBA.

"He gave me this Rolex to remember to always reach for the best. And I do, just not in the way he necessarily thinks the best is. I wear this watch to remind myself of the difference in social class between my father and my mother. One day I'll make enough money for her to live and be treated the way she deserves."

"Wow, that's an amazing story behind your watch. Your mom sounds like a strong lady."

"She is. I want you to meet her one day."

LaMonica and Coby continued to talk over the next hour. He led most of the conversation. Not in a controlling way, but in a confident manner.

Coby seemed to know himself quite well. His likes and dislikes. His goals in life. LaMonica thought how nice it would be to know yourself like that. She had become an adult early in life by becoming responsible for another person, yet when she thought about it, she really didn't know much about her own self at all. Not like Coby. Maybe one day she would.

After Coby left LaMonica asked Mama, "So Mama can Coby start coming over on the weekends?"

"Sure. I guess. I mean chile, you ain't married to nobody."

Yep, Coby had won her over.

At school, LaMonica and Coby began spending time with each other at his apartment in between classes. He'd often order in Chinese food for lunch. They got to know one another on deeper and deeper levels and poor Coby still had no idea LaMonica was in a live-in relationship with her child's father.

Soon Coby wanted her at his games.

"I can give you some gas money to give your friends if they can give you a ride to my games."

Jacqueline had moved in with Big Jimmy at this point. They would give her rides to Flint to watch college basketball games. They had no idea, though, that she was in a relationship with one of the players. As far as Jacqueline and Big Jimmy were aware, LaMonica was in a relationship with Bishop and him only.

LaMonica attended these games out of support for Coby. She knew absolutely nothing about the game of basketball and had little interest in it. Often Coby's teammates' girl-friends would have to tell her when it was time to cheer.

"Girl, you'd better clap for your man. Didn't you just see what he did on the court."

"Oh, yeah!" LaMonica would reply and then clap on cue. Coby was often checking to see if she was paying him any attention.

One day his father showed up and surprised Coby before the game. Coby introduced LaMonica to his father.

"Dad, this is my girlfriend LaMonica."

"Wow, she's beautiful.

"So that's why I haven't heard from my son you've been keeping him busy."

They all laughed.

LaMonica and Mr. Sway sat together in the bleachers. Some of the teammates' girlfriends were on the step team and they put on a great show before the game.

LaMonica and Mr. Sway watched Coby play. Mr. Sway was really into the game. He was happy when Coby made baskets and upset whenever he felt the referees had made a wrong call.

Jordan College won and Mr. Sway wanted to take LaMonica and Coby out to eat, but she knew she was pushing her luck with going home so late. Besides, Jacqueline and Big Jimmy had stayed at the mall in Flint to give her a ride home.

"I'm sorry I have to get home, Mr. Sway. Maybe next time."

"Definitely next time. I'll be coming back to see Coby play. That coach is going to have to give him more playing time on the court."

When Big Jimmy dropped LaMonica off, she had him stop at the local liquor store instead of taking her all the way home. She didn't want Bishop to see who had dropped her off or have questions about where she had been.

"You can just let me out here."

It surprised Big Jimmy LaMonica wanted to get out at a liquor store.

"You be careful out here, young sista."

"I will."

8

GOING OUT

LaMonica had been lucky. Bishop had been so caught up in whatever activities he was doing outside of the house that he hadn't noticed her comings and goings. But he did notice how far apart they were becoming physically.

LaMonica's heart had become far away from Bishop now. She was falling for Coby, and there was no room in it for Bishop anymore. Coby had shown her how a woman should be treated.

He had continued to visit her on the weekends at Mama's house. Each time coming with a single rose for her and a single rose for Mama. He would often give her presents she had to hide. He had even given her money on a bill.

Bishop had never paid a bill in all the years they had been together. How could she respect that?

Bishop could feel that something was wrong between him and LaMonica.

"Baby, we need to spend more time together and have fun again. How about you invite Jacqueline and her man over for cards instead of washing at yo' mama's house this weekend?"

"Okay, I'll call her up and make the plans."

This would mean LaMonica would have to find some sort of excuse to not have Coby come down for the weekend. Believe it or not, she was a horrible liar under normal circumstances. She didn't know how she had survived being a player of hearts all these months since school started.

As luck would have it, Coby had an away game, and she was home free.

Jacqueline and Big Jimmy came over for game night. After a few rounds of cards and dominoes, they suggested they all go out riding.

"Bet that!" Bishop said.

"LaMonica, see if Jessica (the roommate) can watch Monica."

"I don't know Bishop, I don't like really leaving her with people."

"She's not just people LaMonica. We know her. Besides, she watched Monica before, and it was fine. Baby, the girl don't pay no rent, she can at least watch the baby for us."

"Well, let's wait until I can get her to go to sleep."

After LaMonica got Monica off to sleep, everyone headed out in Big Jimmy's car.

Jacqueline and her boyfriend were in the front seat, and Bishop and LaMonica were sitting in the back. This was as close to a date as they had had in a very long time.

"Aye Big J, you wanna run by the liquor store so we can grab some dranks?"

"Sure brotha."

Bishop ran into the nearby liquor store and grabbed some red plastic drinking cups for everyone in the car, along with some dark liquor and cola.

LaMonica had to keep her lip from doing an Elvis Presley impersonation. She forced a smile as he passed her a drinking cup. *It's funny how Bishop has money for things like this but nothing else*, LaMonica thought.

"So, where we ridin' to?" Bishop asked.

"I thought we'd hit some of the spots around here. And if we ante up on some gas money, we can shoot down to Flint to see what they got goin' on down there."

"Oh yeah, fa show my nigga, fa show. Bet that. I got you. I got 10 on it. Will that do?"

"Definitely young brotha. One love."

They rode around hitting the same spots LaMonica and Marciana did back when it was her birthday. Young people who lived on the East Side of the river in Saginaw didn't have many choices for entertainment.

First, they rode up and down East Genesee Street. Then they stopped at 7-11 and parked with the other cars. Bishop and Big J knew a lot of people out there. Someone was constantly stopping by the car window and giving Bishop dap. Other people sitting in cars were getting out and doing the same thing with friends they spotted. Some car parkers were having loud conversations with people parked to their left and their right.

The store owner didn't seem to mind his parking lot being used as a makeshift club spot. It brought him constant business of people coming in buying cigarettes, liquor, and papers to wrap marijuana in. But the police didn't like people congregating like that because it often ended up with fights or gunfire.

"Aye, bump the music a little bit, Big J," Bishop said.

Bishop was feeling good turning up his drink.

"Aye baby, why you ain't drinkin'?" He smiled over at LaMonica and tried to pour her some of his liquor.

"I'm okay."

"What? Nawl we're supposed to be havin' a good time."

"I don't like that dark liquor, Bishop. It's too strong I can barely swallow it."

"Awe yeah, you a lightweight. I should have known better. Let me run in here and grab you a wine cooler or somethin'."

"I'll come too. Jacqueline, you want some coolers?"

"Yeah baby," Jacqueline said.

Bishop and Big Jimmy went in and grabbed coolers and cigarettes. They both smoked heavily. LaMonica thought about Coby, how he didn't smoke. He had once told her he could never again kiss a girl who smoked. "I tried it once, that taste was awful. It was such a turnoff," he had said.

LaMonica agreed. When she thought back on it, every time she had engaged in a deep kiss with Bishop it tasted like cigarettes. When she was deep in love with him it didn't bother her at all. Part of his bad boy image. A character plus in her opinion.

But now she found it sickening. He smoked so much the taste wasn't just on his tongue. It was on his lips, his fingers, his clothes, everywhere.

Bishop and Big Jimmy had returned. Soon he and Jacqueline were in the front seat, kissing.

"Come here, baby. Get closer to me. Why are you all the way over there?" Bishop asked.

Bishop had continued to scoot closer and closer to LaMonica in the car. When he was drinking and not paying attention, she would inch away from him bit by bit.

"What I'm right here. We're in the same car, Bishop," she whined.

Bishop had thrown back the dark liquor a few times now. He wanted to get cozy. LaMonica scooted near him as he asked. He put his arm around her and there it was again, that tingling feeling. Not in a good way. Everything in her said, "stop." She couldn't stand him being that close or even touching her anymore. She tried to hide it, but on reflex she flinched and moved back.

"What's wrong with you?" Bishop asked.

The look on LaMonica's face showed absolute disgust. Her lip kept involuntarily curling up and her nose was crinkled as she cringed away.

"Oh, you don't want me to even touch you?"

"No, no, I was just...... trying to get comfortable."

"Alright then. Don't be actin' funny!"

LaMonica pushed herself to remain close to him and let him put his arm around her. It was a real mental job. She realized (other than going to sleep at night) she hadn't been this physically close to him in a while. It caused some sort of sickening feeling inside of her.

She didn't know how other females did it. Keep two boyfriends at the same time. She now cared for one and couldn't bear to be near the other.

9

THE HOE STROLL

A s they got closer to the I-75 highway headed for Flint, Bishop leaned in for a kiss and LaMonica moved quickly to the far side of the car near the door.

"What the hell is goin' on LaMonica?" Bishop shouted. "Who you messin' with? Cuz you gotta be messin' with somebody."

"What? Bishop, I just don't feel like all of that."

"Oh, hell nawl! I ain't crazy LaMonica. You don't want nobody to touch you or nothin'. Somethin' is going on."

Big Jimmy stepped in after all of Bishop's yelling. "Okay, hold on, young brotha. You can't be yellin' at her like that."

"Look man, this is my woman. I'm handling this back here."

Jacqueline could see the two men were headed for a serious disagreement. "Just scoot over there by him so everyone can calm down," she whispered.

LaMonica complied. She scooted over next to Bishop again.

He wrapped his arm around her. "I don't know why you was trippin' anyway."

"It's just hot in here and smokey Bishop. It's not making me feel right. That's all."

"Okay, I'm sorry for yellin' at you. You know you're my baby," Bishop said.

Then he tried to kiss her again. LaMonica flinched and moved her head back. She just couldn't help it. To lock lips or even worse tongues with Bishop would make her stomach turn.

Bishop was punching the back of Big Jimmy's seat. He spoke harshly to LaMonica with every beat. "You know what? Now I know you effin around now. Now I know it. After all this time. I can't believe you."

"Why are you back there yellin' at her like that again?" Big Jimmy jumped in.

"Don't make me pull this car over. That might be how you talk to yo' woman at home, but you ain't gonna talk to her like that around me!"

Now Bishop was feeling disrespected that Big Jimmy was getting in his business. "Pull this car over then, nigga. Pull it ova. Cuz this is between me and my woman."

"Nawl, you look here youngin'. I've been knowin' LaMonica since she was a little girl and I know her mama, Mrs. Powers, too. And you ain't gonna talk to her like that while I'm around, young brotha."

Big Jimmy took the exit off I-75 to a gas station in Beecher, which was minutes before Flint.

"Let's get some gas and let me talk to you, B."

Bishop and Big Jimmy got out of the car. Jacqueline immediately turned to LaMonica. "Girl, why don't you want Bishop to touch you?"

"I don't really wanna be with him anymore Jackie, to be honest. But I'm trying."

"Well, just let him put his arm around you or something. Because otherwise if he keeps yelling at you, he's gonna piss off Big Jimmy. And I'm afraid they're going to get into a fight."

"Okay." LaMonica agreed. But she couldn't push out of her mind the stark contrast between Coby and Bishop.

It just kept rolling around in her thoughts that for all these years Bishop had been telling her she wasn't a "real woman" when in truth it was him who wasn't *a real man*. And now she had someone to compare it to.

It was really funny to her how Bishop could come up with money for drinks and riding around for a fun weekend night, but he couldn't come up with not a dollar for a bill or a toy for his own daughter. Not even a birthday present. Yet this man Coby, who was just a college student and didn't owe her anything, had done more for her and her baby than the entire 3 years she had known Bishop.

Coby had asked her about her child's father. Of course, she spoke of him as someone from her past. She explained his criminal behavior and how he always made her feel like she wasn't good enough. Like she wasn't making the cut as a woman in his life and calling her a teeny bopper.

"Well, LaMonica you were, you were a teenager. And he had no right expecting those things out of you."

That truth had slapped her across the face like a Mack Truck. She had been so busy trying to be grown, trying to get out of Mama's house that she didn't realize until she was an adult that she had never been one before.

The truth was, she had been a teenager who, through education and work, had tried to become the best version of an adult she could be and to take care of their child. Lord knows she couldn't rely on Bishop to help with any of that.

LaMonica had no plans on acting on her feelings. She planned on staying with him, for Monica's sake. But in all honesty, what could Bishop do for her now? Except nauseate her. It was like a veil of smoke had been lifted from her eyes. Now that this truth was clear, she couldn't unsee it.

Big Jimmy and Bishop had a heart to heart and then put gas in the car. Everything seemed to have calmed down between them. LaMonica was a horrible actor. But she would try to act affectionate with Bishop and get them through this night. Because she knew all too well how easily conflict could escalate.

They were riding down Saginaw Street when Beecher crossed over into Flint. Everyone was out and about because it was a weekend night. People had parked their cars and were walking up and down the sidewalk on both sides of the street.

"Man, we gotta find us a place to park and get out," Big Jimmy said with excitement.

"Yeah man. No doubt. It's all the way live out here tonight." Bishop responded.

They made it to downtown Flint and rode past the Copa Club. Now there was a memory. Just months back LaMonica had attended this club with Bishop in anticipation of watching her older brother Alvin perform.

Alvin wasn't around much because he had a music contract with Atlantic Records and was often on the road making music. Last year he came to Flint with the popular R&B music group, Silk.

Everyone in LaMonica's family was excited about seeing Alvin perform alongside this group. She had made it there with Bishop. After watching him perform, Alvin walked over to her with excitement. He was being managed by the famous singer Eddie Levert.

"I'm glad you were able to get in. The crowd was so big tonight they turned a lot of people away."

"Oh, we came early. There was no way I was gonna miss you." LaMonica said.

"How you doing, man?" Alvin stretched his hand out to Bishop, and they shook hands.

"Hey, let me introduce you to some of the guys."

Alvin brought LaMonica and Bishop over to the VIP area and one of the world famous members of Silk came over.

"This is my sister, LaMonica." He stretched his hand out to shake hers.

Bishop intervened and in a LOUD whisper said, "You'd better not shake that man's hand!"

She was shocked. But obediently she snatched her hand back and the star awkwardly pulled his hand back as well and left. Alvin was mortified. He had always warned everyone in the family not to embarrass him in front of people from the music industry.

LaMonica just felt controlled.

Eventually every controlled creature will try to escape unless they've become conditioned like a scientist's experimental dog. One day LaMonica would get the chance to test that theory on her relationship with Bishop. One day soon!

They pulled over to park and LaMonica realized they were only a few blocks from Coby's apartment. *What if someone sees me out here with Bishop from college?*

Mainly people in her age group were outside downtown. Everyone hung out on Saginaw Street on the weekends. You could see people walking from restaurant to restaurant and from pub to pub. The last thing LaMonica needed was for someone who knew her and Coby to recognize her.

Look at all these young college aged Black people out here, buying things in the tents and booths, and dressed nice for the weekend. This is like the one spot everyone goes to in Flint. Someone from Jordan College is bound to see me for sure.

The more LaMonica worried about someone seeing her, the more her fear turned to irritation at Bishop.

Just as everyone was about to exit the car and check out the music and sights on Saginaw Street, Bishop came towards her for a kiss. LaMonica flinched and moved in an instant.

"You know what you can't tell me, you ain't a hoe! This girl ain't nothing but a hoe!" Bishop said with fury.

"Okay now hold up partner, you ain't gonna be sittin' here callin' Mrs. Powers' daughter no hoe. I done seen plenty of hoes in my day and she ain't one of 'em."

"That's right Bae, tell him. I've listened to you back there hollering at my girl in the car for a while now. And she ain't even saying much back to you. But you've done crossed the line now. B you ain't gonna just keep sitting up here callin' my friend no hoe. LaMonica's been a good girl to you starting from way back in high school," Jacqueline said.

"If you think LaMonica's a hoe, then you don't know what a hoe is!" Big Jimmy added.

"She doin' somethin'. All of a sudden she doesn't want me to touch her, kiss her, hold her, nothin'. Hell, she doesn't even want me to put my arm around her. If she ain't letting me touch her, then somebody else must be and that makes her a hoe."

Big Jimmy started the car up.

"Where are we going?" Jacqueline asked.

"I'm about to help this young brotha know what the true definition of a hoe is."

"What?" Jacqueline asked, halfway ignoring Big Jimmy because his response didn't make any sense.

"Look Bishop, my friend is not a hoe. I've been knowing LaMonica ever since we were little girls. She's always been the type to look out for other people. When I was a little girl her and her mama used to take me to carnivals and out to eat. I didn't have no money. My mama was gone, and my daddy mistreated us all. I didn't have nothin' and LaMonica and her mama treated me like family.

"Then when we got in high school, and she came over to Saginaw High, she treated me the same way. I didn't have name brand clothes like she did, and the rest of the students in school. Everyone at school mocked me, but she was still my friend.

"I talked to a lot of boys at the same time. Some of them were supposed to be my boyfriends, and some I was just having fun with.

"Niggas always have been trying to holler at her when we're out and about and she always tells them the same thing, 'I've got a boyfriend.' Even my boyfriends used to ask me, 'Why can't you be more like your friend LaMonica and stop giving dudes attention?'

"Shoot, when we're in the hood and walking, if dudes try to holler at her, she doesn't even give them the time of day. It doesn't matter how nice their car is or how much money they have, she won't even tell them so much as her name. She says, 'I have a boyfriend' and keeps it movin'. So, I ain't fixing to sit up here and let you call my friend no hoe."

"I know that's right, baby." Big Jimmy said.

Big Jimmy looked Bishop over. Even after Jacqueline's big speech, he didn't look convinced. "Okay, I'll tell you what, partner. You look at this young lady and see her as a hoe, huh? I'm gonna show you what a hoe is. We're going out on the hoe stroll in Bay City so you can see what a hoe really is."

"No Big Jimmy, come on. Don't do that," Jacqueline anxiously pleaded.

"Nawl, nawl I'm gonna show him what's up tonight."

Now Jacqueline was upset with LaMonica. She turned around in her seat. "See, why couldn't you just let him touch you? Now my man's going out on the hoe stroll."

LaMonica placed her forehead in her hand. This whole scene had gotten way out of control.

LaMonica was completely wowed that Jacqueline had taken her side. No one had ever stood up for her like that. And everything Jacqueline said had been true up until she met Coby. LaMonica felt guilty for that part.

Bishop had hyped Big Jimmy back up by disrespecting her again. He was now back on I-75, heading back to Saginaw.

"Where we goin'?" Bishop asked.

"We're gonna drop the ladies off and I'm gonna show you what a real hoe looks like, like I said. Because obviously you've got the wrong definition of a hoe, my brother."

"Wait what? You were serious? Come on Big Jimmy, I don't want you doing that."

"Nawl, nawl, I need to show the young brotha LaMonica ain't no hoe. We're going down to the hoe stroll and I'm gonna show you what a real hoe looks like, B."

"Alright. Bet that!" Bishop responded.

"See, girl, why you couldn't just let him kiss you and touch you? They're really doing it!"

LaMonica didn't care that much. This whole lesson on hoes seemed illogical, anyway. At this point she felt like she didn't care what Bishop did. At least he was going to stop bothering her for the rest of the night. She felt sorry for Jacqueline, though.

In the back of her mind, LaMonica didn't take what Big Jimmy was saying too seriously. She figured he had kicked back a few drinks, but by the time they made it back to Saginaw, he would just go home with Jacqueline.

Nope.

Surprise, surprise. Big Jimmy dropped Jacqueline off and came back for Bishop for his ghetto training on *how to tell the difference between a lady and a tramp.*

10

THE TRUTH WILL SET YOU FREE

Bishop didn't return until the wee hours of the morning. He climbed in the bed. "Hey. Hey baby, you up?"

"I'm sleep Bishop. What time is it?"

"It's around 4 a.m. Look baby, I just wanted to let you know I didn't go out lookin' at no hoes. I just wanted to hang for a minute."

"So, you didn't really go on the hoe stroll, Bishop?"

"Nawl baby, of course not! Me and Big Jimmy talked. But more importantly, I had time to reflect. And baby, I know what Jacqueline said was true. I know everythang that hoe said was right. Everybody knows how she is out there. Out there like a hoe. And even though y'all are friends you ain't neva been the same as her. When she said, 'All my boyfriends said I should be more like LaMonica,' I knew that hoe was tellin' the truth baby and I'm sorry. We're gonna get our relationship right again baby."

"Okay, Bishop."

And with that they went to sleep, not knowing that one phone call in the morning was about to change everything.

LaMonica woke up the next morning taking care of Monica and getting ready to cook a nice Saturday breakfast when the phone rang.

It was Big Jimmy, and he was really hyped up.

"Look here LaMonica I had to call you this morning and tell you that nigga Bishop ain't who you think he is."

"What do you mean?"

"Look LaMonica, I've got a lot of respect for yo' Mama and I think you're a nice girl. That's why you need to get away from that nigga."

"What are you talking about, Big Jimmy?"

"Last night he was smoking a crack rock in my car."

"What!" LaMonica exclaimed.

"Yeah, we was riding down the street chillin' and he pulls out a rock, wanting me to smoke it with him. I told him, 'I don't do that. Man, that's what the old me used to do.'

"LaMonica, it took me a long time to get off that crack rock and I don't mess with it. Baby girl, you need to know who that nigga really is."

Bishop could tell something was up with the way LaMonica was responding to the phone conversation. She was on the phone in the living room and Bishop was still in the bedroom.

"Baby, who you own the phone with?" Bishop hollered out.

"Listen LaMonica, I ain't scared. Tell that nigga what I said."

"Bishop Big Jimmy says you tried to get him to smoke crack last night, and that you were smoking it."

"Baby, that nigga is lyin' to you. I don't know what his end game is, but that nigga is lyin'."

"He says you're lying," LaMonica told Big Jimmy.

"LaMonica baby girl, I ain't got no reason to lie to you. I

think you're a good girl. You're going to school, you're trying to better yourself, and Mrs. Powers raised you right. I'm just tellin' you baby girl because you deserve better than this."

Bishop was still in the bedroom, but yelling out. "That nigga is lyin', baby. I bet you he won't say that to my face."

"Big Jimmy, are you willing to say what you just told me if Bishop picks up the other phone?"

"Hell yeah. I ain't got no problem with it. Tell him to get on the other phone."

"Bishop, can you pick up the phone in the bedroom?"

Bishop grabbed the phone in the bedroom while LaMonica stayed on the phone in the living room, listening.

"Nigga, why are you callin' here upsettin' my woman with all these lies."

"Don't play with me, Bishop. You know you pulled out that rock and tried to get me to smoke it. I ain't got no problem admitting I used to have an issue with drugs, but I got myself straight now and you need to do the same. You need help! And LaMonica deserves to know what you've got her in the middle of."

Bishop got loud with Big Jimmy. If he could have reached through the phone, he would have punched him. "Nigga, you ain't neva seen me with no crack rock! You can get off my phone lyin."

Bishop hung up on Big Jimmy. The line stayed connected because LaMonica still held it open in the living room. Jacqueline jumped on the phone.

"LaMonica, Big Jimmy ain't gonna lie to you. If he says that's what happened, then that's the way it went down. This was the first thing he told me when he got home this morning and we were just waiting for the right time to call you. This is the truth LaMonica."

"I know," LaMonica responded. She told Jacqueline that

because she didn't want to argue with her, but she still held out hope that somehow they were lying on Bishop, and she hadn't actually had a baby with a crackhead.

Bishop emerged from the bedroom.

"Bishop, I can't believe you've been a crackhead for all this time."

"Baby, listen, I ain't been doin' no drugs like that. The only thang I've ever done is weed, really that's it.

"Check this out baby, don't you remember when I was in that accident when Gary tried to kill us both?"

"Yeah, what's that got to do with anything, Bishop?"

"Okay baby, I'm gettin' to it. Listen, whenever somebody has an accident like that they check 'em for drugs. If I would have had drugs in my system, they would have locked me up. You see, they kept Gary."

"Okay Bishop. We're gonna get to the bottom of this. Let's call down there to the hospital right now!"

"Fine baby. You can call the hospital. You can check."

LaMonica looked up the phone number for St. Mary's Hospital in the yellow pages. The floor workers there were about to get the highlight of their day and didn't know it.

After a bunch of transferring LaMonica was finally connected with the floor that treated Bishop. The operator who transferred her had already somewhat prepared the floor unit secretaries for her request. She wanted Bishop Holmes' records of the night of the accident, and specifically she wanted to know if they had tested him for drugs and if he had drugs in his system.

The HIPPA law which prevents medical information from being given out had not yet been enacted and wouldn't be for a few more years. The hospital had simple verbal agreement protocols in those days.

"How can I help you, ma'am?"

"I need to know if Bishop Holmes was tested for drugs on the night of his accident."

"I understand that. But we can't give that information out without his permission."

Bishop was listening in next to LaMonica on the cordless phone.

"Well, he's standing right here next to me and he's on the other phone."

"Say something Bishop!"

"I'm here. This is Bishop Holmes."

The floor unit secretary asked Bishop for his date of birth and social security number. He gave them all the information.

"Okay, I have your lab results on the screen."

"What are they?" LaMonica impatiently asked.

"The request has to come from him. He needs to say it."

"Bishop Holmes?" the floor unit secretary asked.

"I'm here."

"Sir, do we have your permission to read out your record?"

"Yes," Bishop nervously answered.

"Okay, well, I see you were here that night and admitted for injuries you sustained from a car accident. Is that all?"

"No, that's not all," LaMonica jumped in. "Were there drugs in his system when he came in?" She needed this information pronto!

"Again, young lady, he has to ask me that, not you."

"Ask her Bishop! Ask her!"

"Sir, do you want me to go over your labs on the phone?"

"Yes," Bishop responded.

"Alright well, we ran several medical labs on you, but a drug screen wasn't one of them since you were the passenger. That's something we typically only do for the driver of an accident. But since we've been on this phone call, the unit doctor has become interested in your situation. We think we have a solution for the both of you. If you come down right now, we'll give you a free drug screen."

"Okay, we're on our way," LaMonica said.

"We'll be here waiting." Before hanging up in the background, LaMonica could hear the floor unit secretary chuckling with her co-workers. They probably were looking forward to their arrival for more entertainment.

"We're going right Bishop? Cuz I can hurry and get ready and we can catch the bus over there."

"Yeah baby, we're going. I ain't got nothin' to hide."

LaMonica got herself and Monica dressed. She packed the diaper bag quickly and was ready to go.

"Alright B I'm ready, let's go!"

"Alright baby we can go but check this out... before we leave, I just want to say, you know I be sellin' that stuff so I be touching it... and... it's probably in my system from me touching it."

"Alright Bishop. If that's the case, let me hold some of it in my hand. If people come back with a positive drug test just from handling drugs, then mine will be positive too - and you know I haven't done any drugs." Bishop wasn't expecting all of LaMonica's quick wit that day.

"See you know what LaMonica? I ain't going nowhere. I ain't got to prove nothin' to you!"

And that's when she knew! She finally KNEW! LaMonica looked at Bishop like she was seeing who he really was for the first time.

After LaMonica looked at Bishop like she finally recognized him for the drug addict he was, Bishop jetted up out of the house.

11

THE AWAKENING

I n that one swift action, everything had become crystal clear. Bishop was a dope fiend! And he had been one all this time. All the rumors about him had been true. A flood of memories came flashing back to LaMonica with new context.

There were the times back when he had his car running that he went to dope houses to supposedly re-up on drugs to sell. She had waited in the car with little Monica sleep and strapped in her car seat for extremely long periods of time. Now she knew he was in there smoking crack.

There was the time he took her to an apartment and told her to wait in the living room while he served drugs to a crack addict. He instructed her not to look in the room because the guy was doing drugs. The whole apartment smelled like burning peanut butter. She just kept thinking, *why does Bishop need to be in there with him?* He was in there smoking crack cocaine himself, even then. *I was so stupid;* she thought.

There was that time he pawned Aunt Frieda's radio and told her not to tell. She had never seen that radio again.

There were all those times he was supposedly selling drugs but never had any money.

There were all those rumors out about him using drugs from way back when she first met him as a teenager. There was the embarrassment she had to temper with the compassion she felt for him because of the way he looked and dressed.

She had let it all go over her head because of the tender-hearted sympathy she felt for him. Some sort of nurturing instinct.

This fool has been a crackhead this whole time. He had completely snowed her.

For 3 years she had laid her head down next to someone who she didn't even know, and *that* scared her.

She had heard so much about crack addicts from her family and friends who knew people on it or outright sold drugs. Some people were so addicted to it they would pawn their kids as payment for drugs or use them as collateral. All kinds of things.

In LaMonica's hood, there was talk of a beautiful woman who had become a crack addict. To break her down, the drug dealers made her have sex with dogs for crack while they filmed it. There was talk of that film being passed around all over the hood.

Crack was the worse drug on the street. Once people had a taste for it, they couldn't stop. And they would do anything to get it - scheme, scam - anything! Look at Aunt Felisha.

LaMonica couldn't believe she laid her head down next to this dude every night. She was done. She wanted him gone.

Bishop had left so lightning fast to get away from her accusing eyes, she hadn't had the time to tell him. But she would tell him when he returned home!

Bishop stayed gone all day and didn't return until nightfall. He came in the door with a rush of commotion. His friend Jeffrey was with him urgently saying, "Help LaMonica! Bishop needs help."

Bishop's hand was bleeding profusely. LaMonica didn't know if he'd been shot or what. "What happened?"

"Baby, I was just so angry today I punched a glass window out at a bar."

"Is that all?" LaMonica blew her breath and rolled her eyes. She wasn't about to have any sympathy for him.

Bishop was frantically looking for a towel or a rag - something to wrap his bleeding hand with.

"Don't you see it looks like the tendons are broken in his hand? LaMonica help yo' man!" Jeffrey said with desperation.

LaMonica was done. This failed attempt at garnering some sympathy and feelings for Bishop would not work. This was just another one of his manipulations. LaMonica wasn't good at hiding her feelings in general - they were usually written all over her face. But this time she didn't even attempt to. Jeffrey was awe-struck at just how nonchalant she was being at this situation.

Bishop called the "Ask a Nurse" line at St. Mary's hospital. They advised him to come in for stitches.

"Baby, they said I could lose the use of my hand if I don't hurry up and get to the hospital."

"Oh yeah, well you probably shouldn't have hit a glass window, Bishop," LaMonica said with a sarcasm that he didn't seem to catch.

"Baby, come and go with me to the hospital. Jeffrey will drive us."

Jessica the roommate stepped up and said, "I can watch Monica for y'all."

"Oh no, that's okay, Jessica. I'm not going to the hospital."

LaMonica didn't know what Bishop thought, but she was done with him and that wasn't about to change over his hand injury.

Is he going to make me say it right here in the open? She decided if that was the case, she would.

"Bishop, I'm done with you. You don't remember what happened earlier? I don't even know you. When you get back from the hospital, you can pack up your stuff and leave."

LaMonica was cold in her delivery. She had made up her mind and nothing Bishop did to garner sympathy was going to change that.

"Dang LaMonica, that's out cold! You gonna do yo' man like that when he might lose his hand," Jeffrey said.

LaMonica rolled her eyes as Jeffrey and Bishop left on their way to the hospital.

Bishop returned later that night with his hand stitched up and wrapped in bandages.

"I want you to move out of here, Bishop. I meant what I said. We are done."

"Okay baby dang. I just got home from the hospital. Let me sleep and then I'll get my stuff in the morning."

Bishop went to sleep. In the morning LaMonica resumed her regular activities and went to school. Now that Bishop was moving out, she was ready to go full speed ahead with Coby.

She told him that she had moved out of her mother's house and had her own place now. She then gave him her real home phone number so that he could call her anytime.

They enjoyed each other's company during lunch and went back to his apartment when they each had a long break in between classes that day. This had become their new daily ritual. Coby gave her a 5X7 picture of himself in black and white. He loved to sing more than he loved to play basketball. This was one of his headshots he passed out when he was introducing music industry connections to his music. He looked like a handsome Calvin Klein model.

When LaMonica returned home, Bishop was gone. All of his clothing was still there, though. LaMonica took Coby's picture and placed it on the dresser mirror in her bedroom. Coby began calling her at home after school. She was finally free of Bishop and free to pursue a relationship with Coby.

Bishop called to let LaMonica know where he was.

"I talked to the landlord, and he's gonna let me rent a small basement, studio style apartment over on 9th street. I saw your friend from school, Summer. She lives upstairs baby."

Bishop continued calling LaMonica baby all throughout their phone conversation, even though she had clearly told him they were done. It just didn't seem to register with him. He thought this was some temporary thing. LaMonica just allowed him to carry on keeping the peace. *I guess saying my whole 8 letter name might be too hard for him after all those years of killing his brain cells and smoking crack.*

Oh yeah, her respect level for him had diminished. After realizing he had spent the last 3 years being a dope fiend and lying to her, it was nearly nonexistent.

On the way to school the next day on the bus, Summer told her that Bishop had moved into her basement. *Yeah, I know,* LaMonica thought. But she just let Summer keep talking like this was new information.

Apparently, they both had the same landlord. "Girl, my landlord has a lock on the basement in my house, and that's where he keeps all his tools and his lawnmower for the other houses. Girl, he's moving Bishop in there. I didn't know y'all broke up."

"Yeah, we broke up." LaMonica didn't give the details of why. But she knew Summer had seen her and Coby becoming a thing at school.

When LaMonica returned to Saginaw from school that day after work, she went to her mother's house and caught the late bus home. By the time she made it home, she saw that Bishop had been there. He still had a key. He had ripped Coby's picture in half.

Later that night Bishop used his key and came into the house into LaMonica's room. He had a gun that he kept there in the drawer.

12

BROKEN PROMISES

"**L**aMonica, who was that on your mirror? So that's who you want to be with now?"

"His name is Coby, Bishop. And yes, I'm with him now."

"Why? Why LaMonica? Why would you choose him over me after all we've been through?" Bishop's voice was shaky, and he was crying at this point.

"He's a good guy, Bishop, and he treats me like I've never been treated before. He's in college, he has *some* money and —"

Bishop cut her off before she could finish. "Baby, you know it's not right to choose money over love."

"That's not what I'm saying, Bishop. You've never done anything for your daughter. You don't take me anywhere. You don't do anything for me."

"But our love was so strong, baby. How can you do this?" Tears and tears were flowing now from Bishop's face.

"You said we would never be just baby mama and baby daddy to each other."

And you said you weren't on crack, but here we are,

LaMonica thought. She wouldn't say that to him though because he was pouring his eyes out and so hurt. She may have lost all the respect for him, but she realized not all the love was lost. That was going to be a little harder to shake.

LaMonica was feeling guilty, but she was still holding her ground that their relationship was over. Then Bishop reached into the drawer and grabbed the gun. Tears were all over his face now. "We ain't breaking up, baby. There ain't no way I'm letting you go." Then he placed the gun to his head. "If you leave me, I'll kill myself. I'll kill myself LaMonica. I promise you I will. I can't take this!"

"Ookaaay...... okay! Bishop hold on. Put the gun up." He looked like a lost puppy holding that gun to his head with tears streaming down his face. A flood of feelings were running through LaMonica's heart and head. She had a strong inclination to help him, save him, something - just like when she first met Bishop.

She wiped his tears from the eye that was on the other side of the gun. She looked him in the eye and said, "Baby please put the gun down."

"Are you gonna come back to me? Are you gonna be mine again, baby?"

"Yes. Yes B. Now put the gun down and come here." Bishop put the gun back in the drawer and LaMonica held him.

Still sobbing, Bishop asked again, "Baby, are you gonna come back to me? Are you mine?"

"Yes Bishop. We're back together." LaMonica responded with the only thing that would give Bishop hope to stop his suicidal plan.

"Yes!!! Baby!! Yes! You're mine again!" Bishop said with enthusiasm through a tear-stained face.

The next morning LaMonica didn't go to work or school.

Bishop had asked her not to go to school where Coby was and to spend the day with him. She agreed and stayed home with Bishop to make sure he was okay.

After seeing Bishop so hurt, she was now torn between all the years they had spent together, the fact that they had a child together, and the irrefutable fact that Coby was just a better man than B. He was the kind of man LaMonica deserved. Even Mama liked him, and liking any man was a hard sell for Mama.

Logically LaMonica didn't really want to be with Bishop. His track record was horrible - *was he going to suddenly turn responsible now?*

But her heart went out to him. He looked so pitifully sad and broken to pieces when she said she was leaving him. How could she have the power to make another human being feel like that and use it?

It was a rare clear day in December and so they walked around the neighborhood and ended up at a South Side convenience store that was selling food.

Bishop was buying singles of cigarettes. The store worker noticed LaMonica eyeing the Polish sausage in the window.

"This is something new we're selling," the store clerk told LaMonica. "Do you want one?"

"I love Polish sausages. My mom makes them all the time."

Bishop started scraping around for some change. "Man, I guess I'd better get this girl a Polish sausage."

Ironically the clerk said, "Yeah man if you don't somebody else will."

"Man, don't I know it," Bishop responded with inside meaning.

With LaMonica's decision to leave Bishop, the short of

it might have been Coby, but the longer and deeper root of it was who Bishop truly was and what kind of life she wanted going forward for herself and Monica. Leaving Bishop for another man would just make it easier, or so she thought. She just didn't know how to do that without breaking his heart and being reeled back in by feeling sorrow for him.

Bishop may have loved her in his own way, but now that she had become an adult, LaMonica was realizing he had never been a good boyfriend. Case and point the Polish sausages — it shouldn't have been some epic event for Bishop to buy her a Polish sausage, but somehow it was. You'd have thought he had taken her out for a 5-star steak dinner for all the fanfare he made about it. When LaMonica thought back over their relationship over the last 3 years she could count on less than one hand, the number of times they had gone out to eat without his auntie or mama paying for it.

When LaMonica returned home, Coby called. "LaMonica, why weren't you at school today? Summer told me your baby daddy was supposed to move into her basement, but then he didn't. Does that have something to do with it?"

She tried to whisper to tell him she'd call him back later to talk about it, but Bishop heard her. He grabbed the phone. "Hey me and my girl are together and don't call here no more."

She could hear Coby arguing with him, but didn't know what he was saying. Bishop hung the phone up and LaMonica turned off the ringer on both phones. She just needed time to think. What was the right thing to do? Stay with Bishop, her child's father and the person she had been with since she was a 15-year-old girl or move on with Coby, a college basketball player who looked like a model and treated her good? Did she even have that choice with Coby anymore?

One thing was for sure: she couldn't keep missing days of school and work. She would have to face Coby at school the next day.

The next day LaMonica went to Jordan College to face the music with Coby. She had decided she would confess the whole truth to him that day.

While riding the bus, she was mulling the scenario around in her head. After she told him how she had been lying to him about being single when they first met, he probably wouldn't want anything to do with her. Girls who were closer to his social class were certainly into him at Jordan College. The boy looked like a model. He could get any woman he wanted. He certainly didn't need her drama.

When LaMonica saw Coby at school, to her surprise, he didn't care about the wrongs that she had done. Summer had already filled him in on as much as she knew. Through all of their talks, he was already aware of the kind of person Bishop was.

As soon as she stepped off the bus there Coby was waiting for her. "Let's go back to my place and talk."

They ditched classes and went back to Coby's apartment. "Coby, I'm sorry for lying to you. I've been in a relationship with my daughter's father this whole time and didn't know how to get out of it."

"LaMonica, it doesn't even matter. I'm in love with you at this point."

"I don't know what to do, Coby. He's threatening to kill himself if I leave him."

"Sweetie, I doubt he's gonna kill himself. He's just saying that to hold on to you."

"I have to be honest now with you, Coby. At first, I was

100% sure I was going to leave him. But now, after seeing him crying and pleading for me to stay, it's bringing up my old feelings for him because of our history. I mean I feel so guilty for hurting him this way, and Monica loves him so much."

"Who do you want to be with LaMonica?"

"I want to be with you, Coby, but I'm breaking all the promises I ever made to B by doing that. I'm just not sure of what to do anymore."

"Sweetie, listen to me. Bishop is criminal minded. From what you've told me of his story, he's been that way most of his life. People like that don't change LaMonica. I've got a family member who's been in and out of prison for years and his whole mentality is that of a criminal. Just like Bishop, he's been in and out of jail (and sometimes prison) his whole life. I love him but the man is now 50 years old, and he hasn't changed yet. You'll be waiting around forever for Bishop to change LaMonica because someone with a mentality like that rarely changes."

LaMonica was a visual person and Coby was definitely giving her a vision of her and Bishop's relationship if it continued. She could picture Bishop now 50 years old and still doing the same things. Her still being miserable, struggling to take care of Monica until she was an adult, with Bishop engaging in ongoing criminal activity.

"Listen Sweetie, you're making good steps for you and your daughter, and you have to think about the kind of life you want to have for you and her."

"I agree with you. That's what I've been doing. It's just such a big move to change what I've been doing for the past 3 years."

"Sweetie, I know it's hard, but I'm here and I want us to be together. I even want us to get married someday."

LaMonica had strong feelings for Coby, but if she was honest with herself, she wasn't in love with him - at least not yet. But she would be strong and move forward in a relationship with him. She had to leave Bishop one way or another for the sake of her and her daughter.

When LaMonica returned home from school and work that day, she was determined again to end things with Bishop. She would just have to figure out a way to do it delicately. A way that wouldn't trigger him picking up a gun and threatening himself.

13

FREEDOM RUN

W hen she got home, Bishop seemed to be calm and in a good mood. He had even cooked dinner. LaMonica determined it was probably a good time to be honest and have a talk with him.

"Bishop, when I told you we could still be together yesterday, I just didn't want you to hurt yourself, okay? I still want us to move on."

"You're only sayin' this because you saw HIM today! Baby, we've been together too long to let each other go."

"Bishop, honestly I would be saying this if I had met Coby or not. You're on drugs Bishop and that's probably been the problem this whole time. People on crack will do anything. I just can't trust you."

"Baby, I'm not on no drugs. Baby, I promise you I ain't neva did nothin' but smoked weed."

"See Bishop, that right there. You won't even admit the truth, that's how I know you're not going to stop."

"LaMonica, you promised. You promised we would never be baby mama and baby daddy to each other. Don't you remember you promised that?"

"Things have changed, Bishop. I'm an adult now and I've seen the way a man is supposed to treat a woman."

"So, are you in love with him?"

"No, I'm not in love with him, Bishop, but that's beside the point. In all these years that we've been together, you have never done the things for me he has done or treated me the way he treats me. That's the way I deserve to be treated."

"Why because he has money? You're choosing money over our family LaMonica."

Bishop was just saying hurtful things because he knew LaMonica prided herself on not being a gold digger even though she was pretty. Coby came from a regular middle class background, and he wasn't rich by any stretch of the imagination. His most prized possession was his father's Rolex watch, that he had passed down to him after graduation. But Coby was like most students, living on a budget. He just wasn't flat broke and scheming for money like Bishop.

"That's not true Bishop. I'm choosing what's best for me and our daughter."

"Baby, please, is there anything I can do to keep you? I'll do anything. Please, baby." Bishop was crying again.

Now Bishop had her feeling guilty again because he was once again crying and hurt. Plus, he had made that "gold digger" comment, and that stirred some need inside of her to prove herself.

Now the pressure was on from him to be honest with herself about Coby and the truth was she wasn't in love with Coby. He was just her fantasy guy, the person you go to in order to escape the reality of your true situation. If B would get off drugs, she would try to hold her family together.

"There is one thing you could do, Bishop."

"Anything baby, anything. Just name it."

"Admit you've been on drugs this whole time and go to rehab."

"Baby, I haven't been on no drugs."

Instantly, the compassion she felt for Bishop turned back to anger. If it's one thing she and Mama couldn't stand, it was a liar (okay and a thief, and a dope fiend). And Bishop was all three.

"You know what then, Bishop if you can't admit the truth and change then I'm done."

"I'm not gonna let you go LaMonica. I'm not. I'm not gonna let you go!"

"You can't make me stay in a relationship with you, Bishop!"

"There's only one way I'm gonna let you go-"

Oh my gosh, what is the one way? Is it through death like he sometimes said in bed? Bishop was scaring her.

"-And that's if you look me in my eyes and tell me you don't love me anymore. I'll leave you alone then. But that's the only way."

Oh, that's it! LaMonica thought. *That's easy*. Even though LaMonica was usually a horrible liar, she knew she could pull off telling Bishop this with a sincere look. It was much easier than worrying about him grabbing that gun and doing who knows what.

She looked Bishop directly in his eyes and said, "Bishop I don't love you anymore and I don't want to be with you." Of course, she still loved him, but this had to end somehow.

Bishop broke down in tears and LaMonica left the bedroom so she wouldn't have to face him. She slept on the couch, and he slept in the bed next to Monica's crib that night.

Bishop got up early in the morning and came into the bathroom where LaMonica was getting ready for school.

"You know what? I thought about killin' myself again last night. I was so hurt LaMonica, I grabbed the gun and was holding it to my head again."

Tears were once again coming down his face, but you could tell he was trying to hold it together this time.

"But you know what LaMonica? Do you want to know the thang that stopped me from pullin' that trigger?"

LaMonica had stopped doing her hair at this point. She didn't speak, she just looked at Bishop intently, like she was very curious to know the answer, because she was.

"I looked over and saw my baby in the crib... (Bishop was sobbing and could no longer hold it together) ...And that's the only thang that stopped me from putting a bullet in my brain. I told myself, 'I can't do this, and my baby wake up and find me like this.' Look baby, I see now that you're for real. All I ask is that you let me stay here until I find a place to go, cuz I ain't got nowhere to go."

"I thought you were moving into a studio apartment that the landlord had. Summer said you were moving downstairs into her basement."

"Yeah, well baby that didn't work out."

Most likely he didn't have the money. His house on Norman Street had been repaired but had been taken over by family and they wanted to recoup the money they had put into it to save it so they would be renting it out to paying tenants, not him. LaMonica felt guilty for leaving him and for the fact that Mama messed up his housing situation, so she agreed to let him stay until he could find somewhere else.

"Thank you, baby, don't worry I'm gonna hustle up on some money and find a place."

Bishop continued to flirt with LaMonica and try to win her back for the little time she was home with him between work, school, attending Coby's basketball games and staying late at Mama's house.

She told Coby the truth about the living situation with Bishop. He didn't like it, but said he would be patient with her while she worked the matter out.

Sometimes he would get a ride to Saginaw, and they resumed visiting at Mama's again. LaMonica would have to tell Bishop she was over Mama's washing clothes (which she was) so B wouldn't get suspicious and come over there trying to start something with Coby.

Then there were Coby's basketball games. Recruiters and scouts from bigger colleges would come to watch him play. During one of his more important games, Coby asked LaMonica to come down, not just for the game but for the weekend. Coby talked it over with his roommates and they agreed for LaMonica to spend the weekend at his apartment. Most of them had other plans, anyway.

Coby's important game ended up being on the Friday that Susan had asked her to come in to work at the courthouse, so there was no way she could stay after school. She would have to get a ride back after work from Big Jimmy without Bishop knowing. Coby gave her money to pay for a ride, and they were all set to spend their first weekend together.

Bishop was home watching her every move. Even though they weren't together, Bishop still watched over LaMonica like they were. She needed an excuse and a reason for all her comings and goings.

Bishop's true plan was to stay there and wait LaMonica out. He felt LaMonica was young, and this was just a phase she was going through. Eventually she would forget all about this Coby dude and continue being a family with him and Monica, where he felt she belonged.

LaMonica told the roommate, Jessica, about her plans for getting out of the house for the basketball game and the weekend. Jessica agreed to help her. It was like they were two sisters sneaking out from their dad.

They devised a plan to "take the trash out" and then hightail it over to some of Jessica's friends that lived two blocks over. Mama already had Monica for the weekend and Bishop didn't know these friends of Jessica's or where they lived, so it was perfect.

After dinner LaMonica secretly packed her weekend clothes away and put them in a duffle bag. She went out the back with Jessica shimmying the duffle bag out of view and carrying the trash outside. Taking the trash out was unusual for LaMonica to do. It surprised her Bishop hadn't noticed.

They dropped the trash at the curb and then looked to see if Bishop was looking. He wasn't, so they made a run for it. "Run," Jessica hollered out. LaMonica and Jessica took off running and laughing until they made it to Jessica's friend's home a few blocks away.

This felt so freeing. It was the same free feeling she had experienced back at Mama's house whenever she snuck out with Bishop. But now the tables had turned. Now Bishop was the one she was sneaking to get away from.

14

WEEKEND AT COBY'S

L aMonica called Big Jimmy and Jacqueline and they picked her up from there and dropped her off at Jordan College to watch Coby's big game and spend the weekend.

The energy was high at the basketball game. The Jordan College Steppers came on the basketball floor and did their thing. Some of the girls sat with LaMonica keeping her in the loop on what was going on on the court, because she for sure didn't know. Basketball just wasn't her thing. She was just there to support Coby.

Coby and his team won that night and the steppers told LaMonica there was a college party after. Coby came off the court and picked LaMonica up with excitement. They went to a college house party afterwards. Normally LaMonica didn't go to house parties because of the dangers of gun violence. Bishop had always taught her to be leery of ever going to a house party. "If niggas get to bussin' (ringing out gunshots) you might find yourself trapped or worse."

Lots of people in the hood had been shot or even killed by going to house parties. The hood didn't have fun college parties like LaMonica saw on TV. But Coby and his friends were different. People of a better mind frame knew how to have a good time.

After the party, some of the stepper girls dropped LaMonica and Coby off at his apartment. LaMonica had been getting to know Coby better and better over the last few months, especially since they often left school to be alone in his apartment.

The more she got to know Coby, the more she realized Coby was very much "about his looks." He had face creams, hand creams, blemish creams and even used the same hair gel that she used. He would often comment on her hairstyles, whether he liked them from week to week. And he would offer her advice on how she could touch them up.

With Coby being so beauty conscious, LaMonica had lucked out on not needing to bring any beauty products for her weekend at Coby's. All she had had to do was make it out of the house with her clothing.

Saturday morning when she went in the bathroom to shower and get ready, she looked in Coby's bathroom cabinet for some hair gel. Coby's hair was wavy, and he often held the style with dark protein gel so she knew he would have some.

She opened the bathroom cabinet and discovered two large jars of protein gel. The jars were brown colored on the outside like the gel that was supposed to be on the inside, only that wasn't what was on the inside. To LaMonica's dismay each jar was cleaned completely out of gel and instead there was a bottle of Posner brown toned makeup placed inside.

Hmm, what in the world? LaMonica thought. She couldn't wait to ask Coby about it. *Is there another female that comes* over and uses his bathroom? *Is this her makeup?* It just didn't make sense.

"Coby, I tried to do my hair with gel, but there's makeup in both of the gel containers."

Tilting her head to the side, she asked, "Umm, why is there makeup in both of the gel containers?"

"Sweetie, that's my mother's makeup. She left it here the last time she came to visit me. I'm just holding it here for her until she comes back again."

A likely story, LaMonica sarcastically thought. *Why wouldn't Coby just mail the makeup back to her? And how expensive could some drug store makeup be that it needs to be held on to?*

Coby's answer to the situation made little sense and LaMonica had learned that when something just didn't make sense, there was usually a lie being used to piece it together somewhere.

Why wouldn't he just keep the makeup in his room for when his mom came back? No, this makeup was in the bathroom (in secret) ready to be used. **Somebody** was using it!

LaMonica thought back to some of the things Summer had told her. "You know that sorority girl likes Coby. She's running for the Jordan College Homecoming Queen, and they did an article on her. Let me tell you what it says. 'I'm so thankful I chose Jordan College to study Social Work and now I'm in the running for the college's homecoming queen. All my goals are coming together. It was here that I found that special someone who completes me.'

"Girl, I think she was talking about Coby. Your Coby. I've seen her talking to him."

LaMonica had blown Summer off at the time, she was always coming up with "the juice" on other people. The way she had approached Coby one day when she wasn't at school was mega gossipy "Hey Coby, tell me why is LaMonica's baby daddy now living in my basement? If I, were you, I would find out."

This part of Summer's personality made LaMonica feel like she couldn't trust her and the things she said because she didn't know what her motives were.

But now she was starting to think, maybe there was something to what Summer said about Coby and that sorority girl. After all, she was tall, brown skinned and going to school for a professional degree. She was definitely more in Coby's league than she was.

A thought came to LaMonica, *oh my gosh, she is one of those uppity girls that wears a lot of makeup too!*

LaMonica didn't want to ruin her weekend with Coby, plus she didn't have any proof, just suspicions. She decided she would watch the situation.

~

*A*s the day progressed on Saturday, LaMonica called Mama to check on Monica. Monica was full of excitement on the phone.

"I'm eating fries Mama, fries." Mama had caught the bus and taken her to McDonald's to play on the indoor slide, which was one of Monica's favorite things to do. Mama said things were fine there. She said it was LaMonica's own house she needed to be worried about.

"I was out grocery shopping with a friend and stopped by to check on your house since you're not there. Boy, oh boy LaMonica you really need to see what them folks got going on over there at yo' house.

"That ole sister of ya daddy's was all downstairs in her

robe cookin' in your kitchen and walkin' around like she owned the place."

"Where was Bishop?"

"Bishop wasn't there. I saw that so-called roommate of yours, looked like she was laughing it up with your daddy's sister. What's her name?"

"Felisha, Mama. Her name's Felisha."

"Felisha. Yeah, whatever. Looks like you ain't got nothin' but problems on yo' hands livin' over there at that house on Jefferson Street LaMonica. You need to just leave there and come on home."

"I don't know Mama."

"LaMonica, I can't believe you've now got, not one, but two grown niggas layin' up on you. Cuz Bishop ain't doing nothin' to help you and that so-called roommate of yours ain't got a job either. Hey, I've got another solution for you."

"What's that Mama?"

"You ought to have the power turned off on their tails that'll get 'em movin' out fast."

"Mama!" LaMonica exclaimed with shock and laughter in her voice.

"Whooo hooo," LaMonica and Mama both chuckled about that one.

"But on a serious note, LaMonica you just need to bring little Monica and come on back home."

"I hear you Mama. Let me call Jessica and see what's going on over there."

LaMonica dialed her home phone number and Aunt Felisha answered. She immediately hung the phone up.

Maybe if I call again, Jessica will answer and tell me what's going on.

She called a second time, and Aunt Felisha answered the phone yet again. She hung up.

Why is this woman in my house answering my phone? LaMonica thought.

She called one more time hoping someone else would answer Jessica or even Bishop - anyone but Aunt Felisha.

On that third call, it was Aunt Felisha, yet again. This time she determined not to hang up. She held the phone and just listened. Aunt Felisha had a lot to say.

"Yeah, I know it's you callin' LaMonica. And yeah, I'm in yo' house. I sure am! Walkin' around, as a matter of fact, in yo' kitchen. And yes, I'm cookin' yo' food. Now what? What you gonna do about it?"

LaMonica quickly hung up the phone. Her home was a nightmare. Now Aunt Felisha was outright bullying her. *I'll have to figure something out when I get back because I can't go on living like this.*

LaMonica tried to put Saginaw out of her mind and just enjoy the rest of her weekend with Coby.

He had talked with her a lot about his religion that weekend, urging her to call God "Jehovah." Some things he talked about she could find common ground with him on because Aunt Valerie from Oklahoma was a Jehovah's Witness and had talked a little about them. But many of the concepts Coby believed in were foreign to her and went directly opposite of the teachings she received growing up in the Baptist church.

"Sweetie, think about it. Would you want everyone calling you 'girl' all the time instead of your name? That's disrespectful, isn't it? That's why we call God by His name, Jehovah. Try it."

Coby urged LaMonica to use the name he used for God, "Jehovah."

"Say it, baby. Let's pray now to Jehovah."

LaMonica went ahead and prayed the way Coby was

asking her to pray, but it felt weird calling God a name she hadn't ever used before or heard other Christians (outside of Aunt Valerie) really use.

Coby continued his teachings that weekend. He said it was very important to him that LaMonica learn "the truth" so they could be equally yoked.

"Listen sweetie. I love you. I've told you that before and I want us to get married someday. After college when I finally put that ring on your finger and ask you to marry me, I'll be asking you to be my wife in this life and the next. I love you, sweetie."

At this time LaMonica felt obligated to tell Coby she loved him too, even though she was pretty sure she wasn't there yet. But he was such a good guy, she didn't want to hurt him.

"I love you too, Coby."

"You do? Yes! We're gonna make it sweetie, I just know we will."

Coby explained more of his religion to LaMonica.

- He said hell was translated hades and meant something else, but it wasn't a real place.
- Only 144,000 people could go to heaven.
- But some people would live forever on earth as a paradise (that was the forever marriage Coby was aiming at for them).
- And you had to live a strict life of purity and virtue to make it into paradise.

This sounded way different from the foundation of God and Christ that LaMonica had learned growing up in church. *No hell? No real consequences except death? Only*

144,000 people were going to heaven out of the billions who had ever lived upon the earth? This all sounded very confusing.

The fervor Coby had for convincing LaMonica of his beliefs didn't surprise her. Back when she was a teenager, Aunt Valerie had once taught her that all Jehovah's Witnesses and their children were like this.

Many of her fights with LaMonica's Uncle (who was not a Jehovah's Witness) revolved around whether or not to practice holidays. LaMonica could remember Aunt Valerie being particularly offended by the Christmas tree and presents he put in the house.

Knocking on doors and skipping out on holidays is mainly what she thought of when she thought of Jehovah's Witnesses, but Coby was taking it to a whole 'nother level. LaMonica wasn't sure if she was ready for all of that, but there was no doubt Coby was the better man than Bishop. If this was what it took to be with a better man, she would consider it.

On Sunday Coby went to the Kingdom Hall (where Jehovah's Witnesses worship) with a neighbor from his apartment building. He said he felt he hadn't been living right and had not attended since being in college. Somehow the neighbor had found him and was taking him. He didn't invite LaMonica, perhaps because of some religious rule, but she was content with just waiting for him to get back while she had time to think. More than likely, she would have to make some changes when she returned home to Saginaw.

15

SEASONS CHANGE

W hen she returned home, Aunt Felisha had cleaned out her freezer of all the meat. This was the last straw. Jessica was living with her, not paying any rent, and weeks had gone by with Bishop still laying his head there, too.

Since Bishop was gone more than he was there, Aunt Felisha was running amuck in her house. She decided it was time to get her child and go back to Mama's house. That was the only way she was ever going to be able to truly move on.

When Bishop came home that night, she had a talk with him.

"Bishop, I'm moving back to my mama's house. I can't afford the rent here and it's getting close to Christmas time. I need the money I get from welfare to help Monica have a good Christmas."

"What about us, baby?" Bishop knew then they would definitely be over if she moved back to her mother's house.

"Bishop, there is no us. You know that!"

"Yeah, I see you stayed gone the whole weekend. Well, I tried to mess with somebody else too, but it was too painful.

I broke down crying in the girl's arms, and all she could do was hold me all night. This is hard LaMonica.

"The way you snuck out of here for the weekend, I see there's really no stopping you. You've done moved on. I can't keep puttin' a gun to my head, hoping to change yo' mind. I'm gonna try to deal with it, baby.

"But I just have one favor to ask you."

"What's that Bishop?"

"All I ask baby is that you let the welfare money keep going to the landlord for rent for December. That way I can stay here and hustle. I promise you, baby, if you let that $350 go to the landlord instead of keepin' it, I'll flip it and almost double it. You'll end up with $600."

None of Bishop's hustles had ever made any money that LaMonica could see, and she needed the money for Monica to have a good Christmas.

"Bishop, I was planning on using that money for Monica's Christmas."

"Baby, I'll get it to you before Christmas. I promise."

Maybe it was true what Ms. Demona had always said when she was younger, "LaMonica you ain't got the sense God gave a fool!" or "LaMonica you're just a fool right!" She often replayed every curse that had been spoken over her- unwittingly accepting them at times.

Maybe it was the guilt she felt for breaking apart Monica's family and leaving Bishop, or maybe she was just an airhead, but she found herself agreeing to let Bishop hustle out of the house for a month and keep the welfare money to pay for it.

"Bishop, I'll do it but remember this is Monica's Christmas money."

I mean, this is Monica's Christmas money; he loves her, he wouldn't mess that up, right?

LaMonica took little Monica and moved back in with Mama. Weeks had passed since the Christmas money had been used to cover the rent for the month for Bishop. The days approaching Christmas, Bishop didn't double up her money. Heck he didn't even reimburse her for the original amount - even after knowing it was Monica's Christmas money.

It got to be days before Christmas and Monica still didn't have any presents. LaMonica received her small check from JTPA for working at the courthouse two days before Christmas. She was still without a car and hadn't had any time to plan. Her cousin Olivia was nice enough to give her a ride all over town shopping so that Monica could have a nice Christmas. LaMonica couldn't believe Bishop. This definitely proved that he loved drugs more than anything else in life.

❧

*L*aMonica could see right away that living back at Mama's house would not be as easy as she had thought. Mama had developed her own way of doing things with Monica when LaMonica wasn't around. She felt she knew what was best, and she wasn't about to change her style of taking care of Monica just because LaMonica was around. This is where LaMonica and Mrs. Powers clashed right away.

Monica was missing her daddy. "Mama, I want my daddy. I want my daddy."

"Baby, your daddy ain't s@#$!"

"Mama don't tell her that."

"Well, he ain't."

"Still, it's not good to teach kids bad things about their

parents. I learned that back at Ruben Daniels when I was in high school."

"Look here 'Ms. Powers' this is my house and I run my house. You don't tell me what I can and can't say in my own house."

Mama's using that snarky tone and calling me Ms. Powers again. This doesn't seem like it's gonna go well. The only way this is going to work is if I move upstairs and have some sort of privacy to parent my own daughter.

Mrs. Powers agreed to let LaMonica use both of the apartments upstairs since she was no longer renting them out. But it didn't change much of anything. Often, she would call Monica down the stairs and sneak her bottles, candy, and snacks when LaMonica had put her foot down and said it was bedtime.

She would sing Monica's name out in the old singsong way she used to do back when LaMonica was a kid, and she was in a good mood.

"Moooonnnniiicaaaaa. Come here, Pumpkin Eater!"

Monica would walk down the long flight of stairs.

"Mama, please stop calling my daughter down the stairs at night. I don't want her to end up falling."

"Oh, I'm down here watching her she'll be fine. You don't know what you're talkin' about LaMonica.

"Does she 'Pumpkin Eater'? LaMonica doesn't know what she's talkin' about, does she?"

"Nope Grandma, LaMonica doesn't know what she's talking about."

"That's right, baby. Now come on with me."

"I'm Mama to her not LaMonica. Don't tell my daughter to call me LaMonica."

"Well, you ain't my mama," Mrs. Powers snarkily said.

This is gonna be a real problem, LaMonica thought.

LaMonica continued going to school, work, and spending time with Coby. Now that she lived with Mama, it was easier to leave and do things with her friends and Coby. Mama loved that LaMonica was gone so much. It gave her more time with Monica.

As LaMonica was rushing in and out of the house between work, school, and her new social life, she'd try to have sit-down meals with Mama and Monica, but even those would become frustrating.

"Pumpkin Eater, grab these cups for Grandma."

"Okay, Grandma."

"Now hand one to LaMonica."

"Stop having my daughter call me LaMonica!"

"Well, that's your name, ain't it?"

"I'm her mother, not LaMonica."

"Well, I didn't tell her to call you LaMonica. I just told her to hand you a cup."

"Yes, but you refer to me as LaMonica when giving her directions and you refer to yourself with a title, Grandma. Why is that?"

"Well, I'm her grandma."

"Okay! Well, you should do the same for me."

"What do you want me to do LaMonica?"

"I want you to say, 'pass the cup to your mother'."

"Why? You ain't my mama!"

Ignoring Mama's question LaMonica continued, "I want you to stop handing my daughter things and telling her to 'give this to LaMonica.' And as a matter of fact, I want you to stop calling my daughter down the stairs and giving her bottles and treats when I've weaned her off the bottle."

"Look LaMonica, you don't run my house. If you want to make up the rules where you live then you need to get your own place where you pay rent, cuz you ain't gonna tell me what to do in my own house."

"It doesn't matter who's house I'm in. I'm Monica's mother wherever I go."

"Like I said you don't run nothin' up in here LaMonica. You'd better watch yourself because we both know you ain't gonna whoop my tail. All you are is mouth, anyway!"

LaMonica decided it was best to control herself and not go back and forth with Mama. Eventually, she decided to just ignore most of what Mama was doing with Monica and focus on work and school. But it didn't change.

16

FANTASY VS. REALITY

S ix months later and summertime had rolled around. Little Monica was over 2 years old now and had a well-developed vocabulary. LaMonica received her Data Entry certificate and had completed Jordan College. Coby was still marriage minded, and they were still close. So close that he didn't want to go back home to Illinois during his summer break from school.

Somehow, he and LaMonica came up with the idea to ask Mrs. Powers if he could stay in one of the apartments upstairs during the break. To their surprise, she agreed. Mrs. Powers really liked Coby and what he represented.

LaMonica continued working at the courthouse for the Prosecuting Attorney of Child Support, knowing the funding for her internship could be cut at any day due to her aging out of the JTPA program. Susan encouraged her to apply for government and civil service jobs through the state, city, and county. LaMonica worked at doing that at the unemployment office whenever she wasn't working.

Now that LaMonica was living with Mama, she didn't have to pay all those bills anymore, so she had saved up some money. Mama found a car and LaMonica helped her buy it on a 60/40 split with Mama paying the most. Even though technically the car was registered in Mama's name, LaMonica was of the thinking that they would share it. That would turn out to be not quite the case. This would become a major source of her and Mama's disagreements in the future. But at least for now, getting around was a lot easier and she could now visit with Marciana and her brothers again.

Marciana and Chuck had welcomed the new arrival of their own baby girl by now and they had moved out of Birdie's house into their own home they shared with Malcom near Birdie. This became the new hangout for most of LaMonica's brothers and their friends.

Malcolm would have spades card parties that lasted for days on end. Sometimes LaMonica and Coby would stay there the entire weekend just playing cards. Alvin would drop in between music gigs or shows on the road, and all the brothers would sing constantly. Marciana, Chuck, and Malcolm's home was always filled with music and singing. Coby was talented, but he wasn't anywhere near on their level, and he realized it once he heard them sing. His talent for singing was there, but it wasn't matured and trained so he sounded quite shaky and did a lot of what singers call "runs" when singing.

Once when he and LaMonica were at the Flint Mall, he began singing for the crowd as they walked around. A sizeable crowd of girls began following him with excitement and screaming. LaMonica just looked on.

"Sweetie, I heard the rap group Chris Cross got discovered by rapping at the mall, so from now on I'm putting my pride aside. I don't care, I'm singing everywhere I go."

And Coby did just that. Whenever LaMonica came

home from work, Coby would practice the songs he had been writing all day by singing. He sang in the morning as she got ready; he sang during dinner and when it was time for bed. Some songs Coby wrote were "oh to LaMonica songs" but even those had become hard to listen to because of the abundance of them.

Now that LaMonica had finished her Data Entry certificate, she missed school. Working part time at the courthouse wasn't occupying enough of her time. There had to be something else more productive to do than listen to Coby's singing half the day.

That's when she remembered all the ads she had seen for Tri-City SER Jobs for Progress. SER stood for Service, Employment, and Redevelopment. They had a strong emphasis on helping Hispanics become employable but helped others as well.

After completing an application process LaMonica enrolled in Tri-City SER's Secretarial program. The teacher was hesitant to let her into the program because it had started weeks ago. After giving her a simple typing test, the teacher agreed LaMonica had the typing skills needed to enter the class even after it had started.

SER also offered help in getting a General Equivalency Degree (G.E.D.). Many of the students at SER took classes weekly to build their skills up to the level to take the G.E.D. test. They also took trade classes.

LaMonica was told they would test her level for the G.E.D. and only after scoring in the 90s range would they give her a referral and pay for her actual test.

"You can expect to spend the next several weeks, even months studying and preparing to level up enough to take the actual G.E.D.," the G.E.D. prep teacher informed her.

"This will just be a placement test. Many of the students

score somewhere between junior high grade levels and high school. This will let us know what grade level you need to begin studying at. You'll have to pass the test at the 12th grade level to be ready for the test," she continued.

LaMonica took the pre-test for the G.E.D. and scored in the high 90s. The school said it was the highest score they'd ever had a student get on the test since they'd been training adults at SER for a G.E.D. She didn't need to take any further G.E.D. classes. They would be sending her over to Ruben Daniels with a paid voucher to take the official G.E.D. test.

In the meantime, LaMonica carried on with working at the courthouse and with the Secretarial program at SER while she awaited the date to take her G.E.D. test.

Things with Coby were taking an interesting turn. He had been her fantasy guy, but when he moved in, reality set in. Coby was now there every day, every single day, all day! Most of his savings from school had run out, and he had no money for anything. He wasn't even sure he would return to school in the fall because he was hoping to be discovered somehow by some big music manager.

This scene was starting to feel familiar. No job with only big dreams in the air.

"Coby maybe you should get a job."

"I've been thinking the same thing, sweetie, and I think I found something. A sales position."

"Oh yes, that's perfect for you."

Coby called the job and got an interview. Mama gave him a ride and when he came back, he announced he had gotten the job.

"I got the job sweetie."

"Oh, that's wonderful. I'm so happy for you, Coby. What will you be selling?"

"Knives, baby."

"Knives? Where?"

"Door to door sweetie."

"Wait a minute! Did you have to buy anything to get this 'job', Coby?"

"Yes, I took the last of my savings and bought this state-of-the-art knife set to sell door to door."

"State-of-the-art? Coby you cannot tell me you fell for that."

"Sweetie, I promise you this isn't just any knife set. Look, let me go get the package."

Coby came back with a black suitcase that popped open to a shiny knife set and a pair of scissors.

"Look sweetie, even these scissors are top of the line. They can even cut through metal cans."

"Do you get paid by the hour selling these knives?"

"No honey, it's 100% commission based. I only get paid if I make a sale, but the marketing manager says that'll help me become a better salesman faster."

"Um hmm, and just where are you supposed to sell this knife set at?"

"I'm supposed to go door to door in the Saginaw Township giving demonstrations and taking orders."

"So let me get this straight, you, a 6'4 Black man, is gonna knock on the door of people in the suburbs and ask them can you come inside and show them some knives. Is that right?"

"Yes, sweetie, but you're being so negative. This works. It's been tested time and time again."

"Coby you sound like an infomercial. You didn't get a job, Coby. You just bought a set of knives! How could you get got like that? You used all your money on these knives. How could you be that stupid?"

Coby looked stunned. LaMonica had never called him a name like that before. Tears started falling from his eyes.

"I was just trying to get a job and help out around here LaMonica."

LaMonica had seen Coby cry like this before, back at his apartment in Flint. He had cried real tears over something LaMonica considered insignificant, then.

"I'm sorry I shouldn't have called you a name. I thought you knew about things like this. I should have warned you."

~

*M*ama was glad Coby was there with LaMonica occupying her time. It gave her much more time with little Monica. Often, she would get her dressed and leave with her without asking and often refused to tell LaMonica where they'd been when they returned. It was a control thing. LaMonica noted it but ignored the effects it was having on her and her daughter's bonding relationship.

At Tri-City SER word had gotten around about LaMonica's excellent pre-G.E.D. test scores. The teacher of the Secretarial program was married to an engineer who worked at a company called RC Engineering. They were looking to hire a receptionist and gave the Secretarial students at Tri-City SER a chance.

The office manager, Blair, from RC Engineering came over and explained the specifics of the job. She was a tanned, well-dressed woman in her 50s with short hair. Blair was clearly a woman that was about her business.

After Blair left, LaMonica informed the teacher that she was interested and was given a referral and an application. She was one of a handful of people picked for an interview.

She was ecstatic. So much favor had been poured on her at Tri-city SER. Her teacher pulled her aside and told her pointedly that her fashion for the interview was going to be one of the key selling points - so she had to be top-notch and interview ready.

"You've got all the qualifications LaMonica. You're a fast typist and you have a professional phone voice. I think the biggest thing for this job is going to be how well you dress and present your physical appearance. Make sure to look really well put together, and I'm sure you'll have an edge on everyone else," the instructor advised.

The Secretarial class teacher also told her to get a recommendation letter from the courthouse so she would stand out.

Susan was overjoyed that LaMonica had an interview at an engineering firm for a full-time job. She wrote her another glowing recommendation letter.

LaMonica went and bought a beige two-piece skirt suit to wear for the interview. She made sure her resume was on premium beige resume paper. She knew nobody else would be doing that. Finally, she styled her hair. That's when Coby stepped in.

"Sweetie, is that how you're doing your hair for the interview?"

"Yes. I thought I would just curl it under."

"I know, honey, but you're doing it wrong. I've been watching the way you use the curling iron for your hair and you're doing it wrong sweetie. Your hair could be so much cuter if you used the right technique. You know what here let me do it. Do you mind?"

"You want to curl my hair, Coby?"

"Yes. Let me try to curl it for you."

Awe that's cute he wants to play in my hair, LaMonica thought.

To LaMonica's amazement, Coby whipped her hair up almost as stylish as when she went to the salon. Although after reflecting on it, she shouldn't have been too surprised. Coby had an entire arsenal of self-care products and a lengthy beauty routine.

Whenever they would get ready to go to a card party at Marciana and her brothers' house, or whenever they were invited out to any occasion, Coby took twice as long as LaMonica to get ready.

First, he had to use all his products on his face, then he had to wet his eyebrows and take a special brush to shape them up. Next, he would wave up his hair and finally, he would manicure his nails. Prior to meeting Coby, LaMonica had been the person who took the longest in the house to get ready to go anywhere.

Oftentimes she would remind Coby, "Come on, Coby, we're going to be late! Are you done in the mirror?"

LaMonica certainly wasn't used to Coby's "style." Bishop would never take this long to get ready for anything. And her brothers, even though they were "pretty boys," didn't even have Coby's level of commitment to beauty.

She had even seen Coby cry actual tears about finding blemishes on his face. LaMonica was wondering if it was possible that the make up she found in his hair gel jars was actually his.

17

WORKING 9-5

C oby helped her get ready for her interview and he did an excellent job on her hair. The interview went well. There were multiple interviewees coming and going as LaMonica waited in the lobby for her turn.

When she entered the office there were two interviewers present, Donald, Manager of the engineering firm and Blair, the Administrative Manager for the office staff of both their locations.

Donald stood up to shake LaMonica's hand upon meeting. She shook his hand and immediately knocked over his coffee all over his desk and paperwork. Apparently clumsy LaMonica was back. *Well, I bombed this interview already*; she thought. They both swore it was fine as someone rushed into the office with paper towels and helped clean off the desk. LaMonica handed them her crisp beige resume on premium paper. They seemed impressed.

"Working at the Prosecuting Attorney's Office for Child Support, that's impressive."

"Thank you. I'm an intern but I've learned a lot."

"I see here you've been to college, yet you don't have your high school diploma or a G.E.D.," Blair said, expecting a response.

"Yes, that's true but I'm scheduled to take the G.E.D. test and should have it soon."

"Do you think you could get it within the next 30 days?"

"Oh, definitely I'm scheduled to take the test within the next few weeks."

"Well listen, hun, your recommendations are impeccable. Your teacher says you're the top student in her Secretarial class, and you've interned for a prosecuting attorney. Not to mention the fact that Susan over there loves you. I spoke with her on the phone, and it really came across that she hated to lose you in the office LaMonica and if she had a permanent position to offer you, she would.

"I'd like to offer you the job at this time. It starts out at minimum wage, but we offer 401k and Blue Cross Blue Shield insurance. Are you interested?"

"Yes. Yes, thank you."

Blair, Donald, and LaMonica all stood up and shook hands and with a firm handshake LaMonica accepted the job. It wasn't much of a step up in pay with the hourly minimum wage at $4.15 an hour, but it was full-time, and it was permanent with benefits.

Not to mention LaMonica now had Blue Cross Blue Shield insurance with no deductible, and a 401k. Of course, she did not know what a gold mine those benefits were at 19. She only understood the hourly wage, and that would sway her decision-making process in the months ahead.

But for now, LaMonica was deliriously happy. She had gotten the job. She couldn't wait to tell Coby, Mama, and Susan at the Prosecuting Attorney's Office.

Susan was over the moon with excitement for her. "Oh,

I'm going to miss you, LaMonica, but I'm so proud of you. You deserve it. And you're ahead of the curve. Nineteen with your first full-time job that includes benefits. I'd say you're doing pretty good. Don't worry, hopefully you'll get a raise in hourly pay with time."

Within the 2 weeks LaMonica had before her job started at the engineering firm, she obtained her G.E.D. Life was looking good in all directions except when it came to Mama taking control over her daughter. On days LaMonica was off work, Mrs. Powers would often grab little Monica early in the morning and take her out of the house for hours without asking for permission. LaMonica would look all over the big yellow house for Monica. She could only worry and hope that it was Mrs. Powers that had her until she would return home.

"Where have you been with my daughter all day?"

"Look I'm not a child. You don't question me."

"When it comes to my daughter, I will question you."

"Look here LaMonica I'm not a child and I don't have to report my coming and goings to you."

"But you had my child with you all day. I need to know where she's been. I didn't even know for sure if she was with you."

"Well, where else would she be? Look LaMonica you don't run me!"

"I have a right to know what my child has been doing all day with you."

"Well then, ask your child."

"Monica, where were you?"

"I don't know."

"Monica, I'm your mother if your grandma will not tell me where you've been, then you need to. Where were you?" LaMonica asked harshly.

Monica was on the verge of crying now, "Gone with Grandma."

This is ridiculous. I shouldn't have to get serious with my 2-year-old child to find out where she was. My mother should just tell me.

"Okay baby, don't worry about it."

Mama was taking more and more control with Monica. LaMonica knew she would need to save up some money and get her own apartment outside of Mama's house when the time was right.

As the summer progressed on a gang war broke out between the North Side and the East Side. A family had recently moved from the projects into the rental house next door. Someone had recently shot their house up.

LaMonica's new position as "receptionist" at the engineering firm took on a whole new meaning. She quickly learned that a big part of her duties included deciphering the technical handwriting of engineers and scientists, typing, and editing it and then creating bound science report books.

The writing was full of environmental scientific jargon that she didn't know and extremely hard to decipher. The engineers were usually away out in the field and so catching them in the office to translate what they wrote could prove difficult. This sometimes caused the reports to be delayed because LaMonica wanted to get them accurate.

The whole thing was overwhelming, especially since she had the expectation of simply answering the phones, greeting guests, scheduling appointments, and ordering supplies. You know the things a normal receptionist would do. At $4.15 an hour, LaMonica decided she had to be the lowest paid editor and publisher in history. She found this to quickly become very unsatisfactory.

One day, while editing and typing a science report, Mama called.

"They just shot up all over here LaMonica."

"What!" LaMonica exclaimed.

"Yeah, I had Monica outside with me watering the flowers and a car pulled up. They shot the house across the street and two of the houses on this side of the street."

"Oh my gosh, is Monica okay."

"Yeah, she's fine. A little shook up, but she's fine."

"I guess your friend Coby doesn't know what to think of all this. He said he's never seen anything like it before."

"Probably not. Mama, I hate it over there. It's starting to be way too bad. Don't you wanna move?"

"Girl nawl. I'm not leavin' my house. You sound crazy. They weren't lookin' for me. These niggas know not to mess with me around here."

"Yeah, Mama, but bullets don't have no name on them. Just because they're not aiming for you doesn't mean you or Monica couldn't have been hurt."

"Chile please. I got something for these negroes if they ever let a bullet come flyin' at 1013."

"Okay, Mama." LaMonica was losing patience with Mama's logic. She undeniably needed to move her and her daughter now. But how could she do it making just $4.15 an hour? Now that she had a full-time job, the state had taken away half of her food stamps and all welfare benefits. Her bi-weekly checks amounted to about $288, giving her $576 a month. Rent in a nicer area would cost close to $400 a month, leaving her a minimal monthly amount for food. Plus, to move she'd have to come up with $800, which was first month's rent and deposit. *This is so frustrating*, LaMonica thought. *I'm stuck. Stuck again!*

When LaMonica made it home from work, Bishop

called. He had heard about the shootings over there and wanted to make sure Monica was okay.

"I don't know why you wanted to move back over there at yo' Mama's house, anyway. You see it ain't safe over there."

"Yeah, Bishop, but people get into it with each other all over the East Side."

"Maybe, but not like over there. You know that's the worst part of the city LaMonica. And it ain't gonna get no better. I hear niggas talkin' in the street. They done declared a war on y'all over there. I don't want my daughter over there. Listen, let me talk to my mama maybe I can keep Monica over here with me."

"Monica is staying right here with me, Bishop. I'm not giving you my daughter. But you can come pick her up sometimes."

"I know you don't want to be without her, but I feel like you're being selfish, LaMonica, given how dangerous it is over there. But its yo' call. If anything happens to my daughter, I'm blaming you!

"Yeah, but I'm gonna start pickin' my baby up soon. I'm workin' on putting a motor in a car. I'll have it running soon. As soon as I do, I'll be there to pick her up."

"Alright. Bye."

Bishop had a point. It was dangerous over there. The gun violence plus Mama's controlling ways were more than incentive enough to move, but how? Money was beyond tight! LaMonica decided she would ask for a raise. Blair was located at the company's second site. She agreed to come over for a meeting.

LaMonica was apprehensive, but she mustered up the courage to ask for a raise.

"Blair, I've now obtained my G.E.D. and I was hoping to get a raise."

"A raise? Ha!" Blair laughed right in her face.

"Listen honey, they haven't been too happy with the job you've done over here so far."

"Well, honestly, I didn't realize I'd be editing scientific works. I thought this was supposed to be a receptionist position."

"Oh, honey, you're going to have to learn in life that sometimes you will do things outside of the job description. But not to worry, we're going to be replacing you with a more seasoned professional, and we'll be sending you over to the Court Street site with me. There you'll simply be fielding and patching calls, typing letters, and greeting guests."

Oh, so I'll actually be doing the job of a receptionist, then, LaMonica thought.

"You know, honestly, you weren't properly trained for the job we gave you, so that's ultimately why we're transferring you. We'll need you to stay here until the person replacing you leaves her current job in two weeks. Can you do that?"

LaMonica fought not to roll her eyes and let her face show her displeasure, "Sure," LaMonica replied.

She overheard Blair discussing the new hire's salary. She would receive over $8 an hour. That was pretty good money in the 90s. At least, a person could pay for food and shelter with that and have money left over. *They're paying me $4 an hour and going to pay her double. I bet the person they're replacing me with is White,* LaMonica thought.

To LaMonica's surprise, when it was time for her to meet the new hire, in walked a Black woman. She had worked in administration for years and had much more experience than LaMonica. Working at RC Engineering was her real first job. Everything else she had done up until that point had been part-time internships or paid programs.

She transferred over to the Court Street office where all the bigwigs and Blair were located.

"Blair, if I do well over here, then can I get a raise? I really need to move out of my mother's neighborhood for my daughter's sake. I've obtained my G.E.D. now. I can bring a copy in if you'd like."

Blair had no idea what living on the Northeast side was like. She didn't know about gang wars.

"No, hun, that won't be necessary. You'll receive an evaluation on your performance after a year like everyone else. If your performance warrants you receiving a raise, we'll look at it then."

18

THE BEAT GOES ON

L aMonica desperately wanted to move out of Mama's house at this point. Not just because of the gang wars, either, because of Mama. Her control of parenting over little Monica was becoming unbearable. She was slowly, day by day teaching the child not to love or respect LaMonica as her mother. At some point it was all gonna come to a head and LaMonica wanted somewhere to go when it did.

Not to mention, it was, without a doubt, harder to live with Mama after being on her own for so long. Not only did Mrs. Powers want to parent little Monica, but she still wanted to parent LaMonica too. For instance, at times when she was on the phone talking with her girlfriends Mrs. Powers would get on the other end and say, "It's late and it's time for LaMonica to get off of the phone now!" Mrs. Powers did this as if LaMonica was still in high school with a curfew.

Or whenever Bishop called if LaMonica didn't want to speak with him, she would force her to come to the phone by calling her aggressively. Even though Mrs. Powers didn't care for Bishop, it was a power play. Everyone was going to march to her beat and drum inside of her house.

LaMonica felt demeaned. As a result, she and Coby spent a lot of time at Marciana and Chuck and Malcolm's home. They would often spend the whole weekend there, playing spades and dominoes. Mama didn't mind. She had little Monica, and that's all she cared about.

LaMonica was becoming more and more frustrated with Coby during the week, especially after work. He still wasn't working and when she would come home, he hadn't done anything that she considered productive around the house either.

Every evening Coby would greet LaMonica with excitement when she came home from work.

"Hey sweetie. I've been writing songs all day. I've got one for you to listen to now. *Ooh my love you are my life LaMonica. Nothing can come in between us.*"

Oh, my gosh, could he please shut up! LaMonica was beyond aggravated by the sound of Coby's singing voice.

"So that's all you've done all day is write music and sing? You didn't wash any dishes, any clothes, sweep, mop, nothing-just sing?"

"I'm up here singing a song I dedicated to you, LaMonica. How rude! And besides, I'm not supposed to clean up behind you and little Monica while you're gone. That's not what I'm here to do."

"Frankly, I don't know what you're here to do at all, Coby!"

"I can't believe you said that, LaMonica. We're supposed to get married someday."

LaMonica rolled her eyes and blew her breath. "Humph."

LaMonica went to work the next day thinking about

Coby. He had been her fantasy guy, but the relationship was clearly not working. She had hoped that at some point the lie she had told him (that she felt the same way about him) would at some point magically be true, but alas, it never changed. Her fantasy had been smashed to pieces. She lectured herself, *when you get out of this LaMonica never, ever go out with the "fantasy guy type" again!*

When she returned home from work, Coby caught her by surprise when he said he was returning home.

"I called some of the guys in my family for advice. Most of them told me it's hard for a woman to respect a man when they're in the type of situation we're in. We're living in your apartment owned by your mother. I'm not working. It's just not good for our relationship. I think I should go home and get the support I need from my family, then get a job and we can get our own place or get married later."

Coby was surprised that LaMonica didn't seem upset at all.

"Yeah, I agree. That's the best thing." *What a relief!*

"I mean, unless you want me to stay. Because if you want me to stay, we can try to work something different out."

Ah man, here he goes with those chic tactics again. It was obvious Coby wanted her to say, 'no don't go,' but she wasn't about to do that. Coby had tried these "female relationship style" manipulation tactics before.

Once when they were way out in the suburbs in the car that Mama and LaMonica shared, Coby developed an attitude over some petty disagreement they had. In a flash he had jumped out of the car and began walking down the street with LaMonica following alongside him in the car.

This ghetto romance scenario could often be seen played out in hoods everywhere with one exception—

usually the roles were reversed. The woman was usually walking down the street, invoking the man to show how much he truly cared by riding alongside her, begging her to get in the car. Heck LaMonica had even tried it once herself, but this, this was backwards and a complete turnoff.

Eventually, after asking him to get back into the car several times, she rode off. When she made it home, Mama asked where he was, and she told her what had happened.

"Now LaMonica, you know you need to go and get that boy, he's not from around here."

LaMonica rode back to the Saginaw Township, going street by street looking for Coby for at least an hour. But she could never find him. By the time she made it home he was walking up to the big yellow house on 5th street.

"Did you walk all the way here? Oh, Coby I'm sorry. I tried to come back and look for you, but I just couldn't find you."

"Leave me alone. Don't even talk to me, LaMonica. I can't believe you didn't care enough to keep following me."

LaMonica suspected that's what he was doing now- just trying to confirm that she cares enough to ask him to stay. But the truth was they were better off as friends, and it was time for him to go.

Coby's dad came a few days after that to pick him up.

"I'm fighting back tears, sweetie. The only thing that's helping me to keep it together is knowing we're still together and we're just doing this until we can be together again."

LaMonica didn't have the heart to tell him the truth. Plus, she didn't want to see him breaking down into tears yet again. She decided she would wait until he was back in his own state, and then she would tell him it was over on the phone.

She was thankful for the time she and Coby had shared. Even though he ended up not being her type or the one for her, he had taught her what it felt like to be treated the way you deserved by a man. Thanks to him, she had decided that when she finally was ready to settle down, she wouldn't accept anything less.

∿

*A*few days later, on a Saturday, Bishop pulled up in the driveway. Mama was gone to a rummage sale with little Monica. LaMonica heard him coming before she ever saw him. He had so much bass in his car his music could be heard down the whole neighborhood block.

Bishop got out of the car and was knocking on the screen door of the front indoor porch. He had left the car running with the music blaring in the driveway. He knew Mama was gone, or else he wouldn't have dared do this. LaMonica cracked the screen open.

"Hey what's up baby? I just wanted to swing by here and let you know I got my car running. Just got me some fresh sounds."

"Yeah, I hear them."

"Yeah, yeah. Check out the rims too."

It occurred to LaMonica that Bishop thought he was impressing her.

"You know what, Bishop I'm not impressed by your music or your shiny rims or anything about your car for that matter. If you want to impress me, buy your daughter something. I would find that VERY impressive!"

"Baby, I ain't been out here makin' no money lately. That's why I ain't got her nothin' yet."

"Oh, but you have money enough for rims and sounds on your car?"

"Nawl, baby, you got it all wrong. Baby, listen to me, I didn't have to use money to get this stuff, if you know what I'm sayin'. I got it another way."

"Well, whatever your 'other way' is you could've got something for your daughter."

Bishop looked disappointed. *I thought seeing her today was gonna go better than this.* He hoped since he'd heard from some people in LaMonica's hood that Coby moved out, he and LaMonica would get back together now.

"Listen baby, can I come in for a minute?"

"Yeah, you can come on the porch."

"I heard through the grapevine you got rid of that tall nigga."

"Yeah, me and Coby aren't together anymore."

Bishop moved in close to LaMonica and ran his hand across her backside.

"Hold up, Bishop, that's not cool. Don't do that!"

"Oh, okay baby, my bad."

"Bishop, aren't you even going to ask me about your daughter?"

"Yeah, where is she? I was hoping you and me and her could take a ride in the new whip."

"No, my mom has her riding around at the rummage sales right now."

"Dang, it seems like yo' Mama has little Monica a lot now."

"Yeah, I know. I'm trying to move out soon."

"Well, listen, that's kind of what I wanted to talk to you about LaMonica. I've been reflectin' on a lot of thangs and I see where I went wrong in a lot of instances in our relationship.

"Baby, I just wanna say this, I should have been there for you more when we were together. You were working hard, and I should have had your back better and helped more with Monica so you wouldn't have always had to rely on yo' mother. She half the time acts like she wants to take little Monica from you. I mean, I know how she is. It can't be easy for you livin' with her now."

LaMonica silently agreed with Bishop but didn't think it was a good idea to give him any sign that could cause him to think they were getting back together. So she just listened.

"You know, baby, even when it came to Birdie. I should have had your back better against some of the things she used to say to you when I was around.

"But I know we can't change the past on any of this stuff. I never wanted you to leave me like this. I at least wanted to be able to give you a stack of money to take care of our daughter with if we ever broke up."

"Well, this is where we are now, Bishop. All we can do is just work together to take care of our daughter and do what's best for her."

"This is kind of where it all started, isn't it? Remember our first little date on yo' Mama's indoor porch?"

"Yeah." LaMonica chuckled with Bishop.

"I'll always care about you LaMonica and I'll always care about what happens to you."

"I'll always care about you too, Bishop."

"Can I give you a hug?"

"How about we shake on it?"

They both shook hands.

"Hey, you wanna go for a ride in my new car since Monica isn't here?"

"No, I think I'll wait and let her have the first turn."

"Baby, you know I had to try."

"I know."

"Well, I'll stop by here a little later to see if yo' mama has brought her back yet."

"Okay and make sure you don't play that loud music with my daughter in the car either."

"See, there you go. Bye, baby."

"By Bishop."

THE PERFECT MIX

BOOK 4 COMING SOON!

Find out what happens with LaMonica in book four.

How will she ultimately escape every statistic laid out against her. You don't want to miss the climax to this true life story turned fiction.

Don't Miss the Release Date

Follow Author LaMonique Mac on Amazon

SIGN UP FOR MY NEWSLETTER

Be the first to learn about LaMonique Mac's new releases and receive exclusive content for fiction readers.

www.authorlamoniquemac.com

THANK YOU

Thank you for reading. Reviews are extremely important to Indie Authors. If you enjoyed this book, please consider leaving an honest review on Amazon and Goodreads.

ABOUT THE AUTHOR

LaMonique Mac is an Amazon Best Selling Author. She writes in the genres of Christian, Young Adult, and Nonfiction. She's also a publisher and a writing coach based in "Roll Tide" country Alabama with her family.

The books she has written and published are known for having a southern flair.

She can be spotted coaching new authors on how to write, edit, and publish on YouTube at AuthorLaMoniqueMac.

instagram.com/authorlamoniquemac

facebook.com/lamoniquemac

twitter.com/lamoniquemac